BANEF

RITUAL
AT DYEWORKS

ALI KADEN

RITUAL
AT DYEWORKS

ALI KADEN

RITUAL AT DYEWORKS

BANEFORD BOOK 2

BY ALI KADEN

Edited by: George Verongos

ISBN: 9798387851322

VISIT ALI KADEN'S WEBSITE FOR THE LATEST UPDATES: WWW.ALIKADENBOOKS.COM

AUTHOR'S NOTE

There is no town named Baneford in Massachusetts. Its history, landmarks, and residents are fictional. All other characters in the book are also fictional, although some places mentioned are real.

CONTENTS

CHAPTER 1

THE EXPLOSION SENT tremors through the office, rattling the desks and causing the lights to flicker overhead. Seconds later, looking through the storefront windows, they saw a cloud of dust and smoke rising into the air halfway down the street. Evelyn and the others rushed outside to see what was happening. It was pleasant in the open air, a cool fifty degrees with plenty of light left in the afternoon sky. A group of pedestrians had already gathered around the sizable crater in the road. Evelyn, Trevor, and Cam joined the crowd standing at the edge of where the asphalt had collapsed into a recessed pit.

"Was anyone hurt?" an older woman asked as she approached, hunched over with grocery bags in hand. "I heard it from inside the diner."

A middle-aged man wearing tired workman boots and a faded hooded sweatshirt peered down into the hole. "Someone fell in there," he said. "I think she's dead," he added, shoving his hands in his pockets.

Evelyn noticed blood on the rubble. Through cracks in the rock, she could see hints of skin, and in the corner, she saw the woman's slender arm poking through.

"What happened?" Trevor asked.

"I don't know," Evelyn said, wondering the same thing.

"An explosion underneath the street. It happens," a gruff voice said, as others whispered and murmured around them.

"Something causes a spark, and something else ignites. Boom!"

Cam wiped a tear from the corner of her eye while Trevor continued to gaze down at the crater with his jaw hanging open. Firetrucks and ambulances appeared, sirens screaming, quickly drowning out the chatter.

Evelyn and her colleagues stepped back to allow the responders access. In a matter of minutes, Main Street crawled with clusters of police officers, paramedics, and townies curious to see the hole. The police sectioned it off with yellow tape as the paramedics dug through the rubble. Everyone watched as the responders pulled a woman's lifeless body out from under the debris, put her onto a stretcher, and covered her with a white sheet. The license in her pocket indicated a name that no one in the crowd recognized, probably just someone passing through from a nearby town. Still, it was a sad moment, which the people on the street acknowledged with a collective silence.

In the distance, Evelyn spotted officer Ed Crowley's plump silhouette among the police officers standing by the hole. She waved to him, and he walked out to meet her.

"It's just terrible," he said, taking off his service cap and wiping the sweat from his sloping brow.

"Ed, what happened?"

"One of the underground electric cables. It went off and ignited the gasses under the street. Methane mixed with hydrogen sulfide is flammable and highly explosive. Boom," he said, gesturing an explosion with his hands. "It's a tragedy. They called the electric company. They'll fix it so it won't happen again."

"Do you know who she was? The woman who died…"

"Never seen her before. Just some nice woman from Old Bedford, it seems."

"We heard the explosion from the office," Evelyn said, pointing over her shoulder at the storefront window bearing her company name, EM Realty.

"Why don't you go on inside then? Nothing else to worry about tonight," Ed said in an assuring tone.

"Okay. Thank you, Ed."

"Good to see you," he added, putting his cap back on.

He turned and walked back toward the scene of the accident, which was now completely encircled with yellow police tape to keep onlookers at bay. Evelyn and her team returned inside. When they could no longer see flashing lights from inside the office, it was quiet again. Evelyn and Cam returned to their desks, but Trevor stayed by the window, eagerly watching the street scene as if things were just about to begin.

The three of them were the only ones at the office that early spring day. They'd seen a very busy real estate market that first quarter and everyone had done exceptionally well. For that reason, Evelyn didn't worry about office etiquette or micromanaging her agents that much anymore. Only two days prior, Trevor had marched into the office triumphantly, his blonde hair slicked back, wearing his gray pinstripe suit, announcing he'd signed up four new listings in a week. He pointed to the manilla folders in Cam's hands as she smiled with her hair tucked neatly behind her ears. Technically, Cam was his "team member," which everyone preferred to say, but Trevor insisted on calling her his assistant. She didn't mind. Only twenty-four, extremely hardworking, and the daughter of Vietnamese immigrants, Cam wasn't in the business for titles and accolades.

As managing broker, Evelyn was pleased to know that her other agents, Blake and Sheryl, were busy with multiple clients as well. As a salesperson, Evelyn enjoyed a lucrative quarter, too, with three new listings of her own in March alone. April was coming fast, and the warming weather and longer days always inspired an uptick in real estate activity, year after year. She felt confident her office was ready to tackle that business head-on.

The final hours of the workday ticked by quickly, and shortly after 7pm, Trevor and Cam packed their things and went out of the door together. They exited onto an empty street, with only a single police car parked in front of the sectioned-off hole. Only an hour ago, the street had been uncharacteristically packed with people. Evelyn tried to recall other times she'd seen Main Street *that* busy. Other than the Fourth of July parade, which happened to pass by her office window each summer, Evelyn couldn't think of a single instance, in all her Baneford years, when she'd seen that many people in one place.

Looking around her empty office, Evelyn felt the way she often did in the spring. Every season, when the days grew longer and the weather outside became tolerable, she considered the things she might do if she had someone by her side. She imagined spending time outside, watching sunsets from a dock, and star gazing in open fields at night.

Evelyn was a sight to behold for most men, twenty-eight years old, with a soft face, long limbs, green eyes, and fiery auburn hair. But in her estimation, most men were fragile and hollow, like brittle champagne flutes. She seldom met men with whom she felt a connection, and for that reason, she remained single. She recognized, however, despite her lack of a romantic life, she was blessed. Business was going well, and more importantly, she'd survived. It seemed like a lifetime ago, but it was only a few months since she'd battled real evil *and won*. Only Adrian and Casey knew the story concerning Hendrick.

The name itself used to frighten her—a simple amalgamation of two syllables embodying sheer terror. But she and Adrian had beaten Hendrick, Baneford was safe again, and Adrian had disappeared. At times, she felt as if the whole thing had never happened. In her younger years, Evelyn had longed for excitement in her life, like many small-town girls do. But after witnessing tragedies unfold, feeling the evil of blood magic, and smelling death's putrid stench in the air, she'd come to prefer peaceful over exhilarating.

At one point, the evil had been so close Evelyn feared it would never go away. Yet, in the middle of that terror and chaos, she'd found Adrian. He'd come to Baneford, inspired by only a vision of her. Adrian could see and hear the dead—a gift he considered his curse. He called himself "vrăjitor," which Evelyn learned meant sorcerer or necromancer in Romanian.

When Evelyn was with him, she'd felt the most intense connection she'd ever experienced with a man, and she'd dared to call it love. When the killing stopped and the last drop of blood was spilled, Evelyn had hoped to let go of calamity and hold on to him. That's not what happened.

She turned out the office lights and locked the door. On the way to her car, it occurred to Evelyn she could look down in the hole one more time without anyone getting in her way if only the streetlight would be sufficient. She stepped over the police tape and approached the edge. Staring down, she could barely discern the bottom. *What am I even looking for?* she asked herself before walking away.

In the car, Evelyn felt the need to avoid being alone and decided to call Casey to see if she might like to have dinner.

"Hey, Casey, what're you doing?" she asked, talking loudly on speakerphone.

"Nothing, just hanging out watching television."

"I just left the office. Why don't you come over tonight?"

"Evie, I'm so tired... Why don't *you* come *here* instead?"

"Alright, I can do that. I'll be there soon."

Swiftly changing directions, Evelyn turned the car around, crossed Main Street, and arrived at Casey's building several minutes later. She found Casey in her sweatpants on the couch, leisurely watching one of her favorite childhood movies with a pint of ice cream and a spoon in hand.

"Put that down. We're ordering pizza."

"Yeah, alright," Casey said, putting the lid back on the pint.

"Did you go to work today?" Evelyn asked.

"Yeah, had a few clients in the morning. Finished early and decided to relax," Casey said without taking her eyes off the screen.

Evelyn didn't need to read minds to know Casey hadn't yet fully recovered from the trauma. She'd always been a ball of energy, meticulous with her diet, and driven at work—an elite personal trainer and athlete. Seeing her in sweatpants, eating an ice cream dinner at six-thirty, it was like she'd become someone else entirely. But Evelyn didn't blame her. It was only three months since she'd been nearly killed by Hendrick and forced to witness the gruesome death of her boyfriend, which sent her into a state of catatonia that baffled all the doctors at Old Bedford. Considering everything she'd gone through, Evelyn thought Casey looked pretty good, albeit much less put together than her normal self.

"Are you feeling okay?" Evelyn asked, trying to sound casual.

"Yeah, I'm fine."

Hoping to break Casey's stare at the screen, Evelyn tried something different. She knew Casey could hide her emotions beneath a poker face but could not resist being empathetic.

"I feel awful," Evelyn sighed.

"Really, what's wrong?" Casey asked, turning down the volume on the TV.

"I miss him."

"He still hasn't called, sent a letter, nothing?"

"No."

"I'm sorry, Evie. I wish I could bring him back for you. But maybe him being away means all the pain, suffering, seeing people die again and again, and all the sleepless nights… maybe it means that stuff is gone, too." Casey burst open, sobbing profoundly. Her pain was closer to the surface than it appeared. Evelyn hugged Casey and held her tightly, rubbing her back. The ice cream container slowly rolled from the couch and dropped to the carpet.

"I'm sorry, Casey. I didn't mean to upset you."

"It's not your fault. I think we *should* talk about it sometimes. It's not like anyone else knows," Casey said.

"No, and I don't think anyone else would understand."

"We fought a demon," Casey said, wiping tears from her eyes, a wave of determination flashing across her face.

"Adrian—" Evelyn started.

"He was special," Casey interrupted. "I know he was, and I wish he'd call you, too. Maybe he will one day."

Evelyn smiled at the thought and gripped Casey tightly again, squeezing as much love as she could into her friend.

"I love you too, Evie."

When she heard the bell, Evelyn went to the door to get the pizza and brought it back to the living room. Casey fetched the plates and napkins, and they leaned into the couch and enjoyed a casual yet intimate dinner. They half-watched the movie on the television, going through slices of pizza and chatting. Evelyn kept the rest of the conversation light because she did not want to trigger Casey further in any way. Beyond seeking the company of her friend, she was happy to see the gradual healing taking place in Casey from the wounds inflicted months ago.

When the movie finished and all the slices were gone, Evelyn gave Casey one last hug and headed home. As she drove through the empty streets, her thoughts of Adrian returned, accompanied by a deep longing. It ached at the center of her being. As she approached her building at the bottom of the hill on Mox Street, she found that it, too, reminded her of Adrian.

It was odd to her that the place she'd lived her entire life could remind her of someone she'd only known for a few weeks. After all, this was the street where she'd learned to walk holding her father's hand, the street where she and her mother raced their bikes up the treacherous incline, and the street to which she came home each night after work. This was also the place where her father, Bruce, had died suddenly when she was only a child and the place where her late neighbor, Mrs. White, had come crashing down on the pavement in front of her, meeting her tragic demise.

As Evelyn approached the entrance of her building, she looked up at Mrs. White's empty apartment above hers. The keys were in her pocket as she was entrusted with selling the apartment for her late neighbor's out-of-state son. Evelyn listed the unit a few weeks ago but hadn't received offers. Instead of scheduling open houses, she'd opted to conduct showings by appointment only. That way, she could control who came and went and limit the amount of talk surrounding Mrs. White's sudden death.

Logistically, it couldn't have been a more convenient listing, but each time agents requested a showing for their clients, Evelyn found some excuse to postpone showing the property, essentially blocking the sale. If she were to ask herself honestly, she wasn't quite sure why she did it. She'd always been an ethical and responsible real estate agent. *Do I really hate the idea of having a new neighbor, or am I unconsciously afraid because of what happened here?* she wondered. Fortunately, her client was not in a rush to sell.

Retiring for the night, Evelyn went to her bedroom and found enjoyment in the pages of a new book she'd recently purchased. Unlike the adventure novels she usually consumed, this one was the memoir of global real estate tycoon Hurston Laurent, a celebrity in his own right, known for his shrewd business style and vast property portfolio. Evelyn found his story personal and more intriguing than the quintessential business memoir. Having some relevance to her profession, the real reason she'd bought the book was the glimmer of wisdom in Laurent's eyes that pulled her in. The cover featured a close-up photograph of his face, and that harrowing gaze reminded Evelyn of the refugees she'd seen on magazine covers, fleeing their war-torn countries with huge, sorrowful eyes. Evelyn read the first four chapters that night before falling asleep.

At the office the next day, Evelyn surveyed the room and felt proud. It was an unseasonably warm day, but everyone was there working quietly in single layers of clothing, with jackets slung over the backs of chairs. Trevor and Blake had their sleeves rolled up. Sheryl wore a sundress made of a light fabric and made Evelyn smile because it was an annual occurrence—the excessive shedding of layers at the first sign of spring. Cam had on the same sweater she always wore.

Evelyn took her seat at the front of the office facing the window and watched the street outside as she waited for her computer to power up. Behind her, the office was quiet and remained that way till noon. Engrossed in work, Trevor, Cam, Sheryl, and Blake kept their heads down like students in study hall.

When the concentration broke hours later, fidgeting, blank stares, and the clicking of pens replaced the Zen energy that had previously occupied the room. It was time for lunch. Trevor and Cam left first, walking west on Main Street. Sheryl went to the conference room to eat a lunch she'd brought with her. Evelyn invited Blake to accompany her to the Fairhaven Diner, a short walk from there.

Blake performed remarkably well for most of the previous year, up until his brief departure from the company. Though she'd never learned the truth of why he left, she suspected that he'd come across something nefarious at one of his listings, which she could sympathize with all too well. She couldn't ask him point blank if he'd seen a ghost named Hendrick, but she wanted him to feel supported, nonetheless.

Entering the Fairhaven Diner, they sat down at the counter overlooking the street. Of the dozen or so tables inside, customers sat at half of them, drinking hot soup, snacking, reading, and wasting time. The diner resembled something from a 1950s sitcom, but the customers were extras in a film about the great depression.

"Let me get your lunch. What would you like?" she asked.

"Oh no, please. You don't have to do that."

"I insist. I'll expense it. We'll call it a business lunch."

"Okay, sure. I'll have a turkey sandwich and chips."

Evelyn paid for Blake's meal at the counter and ordered a soup and salad for herself, then led him over to one of the empty tables. As they ate, Evelyn tried to broach the topic of his absence without sounding too inquisitive.

"When you left the office last year… I never got around to telling you; I know it takes a lot of courage to step back and take care of yourself. I admire that. Not a lot of people know how to do that."

"Honestly, I was afraid you'd be mad."

"Not at all. Life is hard. And our job… we both know it looks a lot easier from the outside. I've met people and seen things that certainly made me doubt whether it's the right job for me," she added.

"Yeah." He seemed to clam up at her comment, and she sensed he'd probably never tell her what really happened.

"All I'm trying to say is, I'm glad you came back." Evelyn offered a friendly smile.

"Me too," he said, pausing for a moment to chew. "I guess I don't know how to say this, but I really thought I was losing my mind. One of my Baneford listings last year, it really freaked me out, and I didn't know if it was my mind playing tricks on me or if what I saw was real."

"What do you think now?"

"I think I must have imagined it. The thing is, though, the sellers never said anything, but they were acting strangely too."

"Did the house ever sell?"

"Yeah, it's the one that I closed last month on Seabrook Street. After I left the office, the sellers never got another agent. They just let it sit, and months went by. They called me late January and said they really wanted me to see the house again. They sounded totally different, and when I went back, it was like whatever was there before was gone. No more strange voices, shadowy figures, or objects mysteriously flying off the tables. I know it sounds crazy..."

"I guess some things we just can't explain," Evelyn responded, somewhat confident she'd played a role in his subsequent good luck.

"Exactly."

After lunch, the whole team was back in the office, and Evelyn relished having them there around her. After all the turmoil she'd experienced, she was grateful for any hint of normalcy, even if only at work. For the rest of the day, the hours rolled by effortlessly as each of them worked on their listings and arranged showings for their buyer clients. Sheryl was the first to head out around three in the afternoon.

"I'll see you soon," she said to her client on the phone as she rushed out the door.

At that same moment, Evelyn saw officer Ed Crowley standing in her storefront window, dressed in his police uniform, looking in, cupping his hands over his eyes to block the light reflecting on the glass.

"Ed?" Evelyn said, walking out to meet him.

"Evelyn, good to see you."

"Were you looking for me?"

"Yeah. You got someplace we can talk?"

Evelyn invited Ed in and guided him toward the conference room. As they passed through, her agents perked up in their seats, not accustomed to seeing uniformed police in the office. Once inside, Evelyn placed a cup of coffee in his hands and sat across from him.

"Let me guess! You want to buy a place?"

"Actually, this isn't about me at all," he said. "You remember Mrs. Devonshire?"

"Our third-grade teacher?" Evelyn asked, recalling the Mrs. Devonshire who taught English at Baneford Middle School, where she and Ed first met ages ago. Though he was a few years older, they shared the same teachers at different points in time.

"Yeah, that's the one. I ended up buying her place a few years ago. Small world."

"Oh, good for you."

"I'm here today because, well, I'm not sure you're aware, but our mayor happens to be my cousin."

"Marty Jenkins is your cousin?" Evelyn asked with a bit of astonishment in her tone.

"Yeah. First cousin on my mother's side. Anyway, he's up for reelection soon, and he's working on something big for the town. There's this well-established developer looking to buy and renovate our old mill buildings. They want to start with Dyeworks," Ed said, gesturing in the direction of the industrial district.

"That's good to hear! It's about time the bigger developers come to Baneford."

"Exactly. Marty asked me if I knew any good local real estate agents, you know, anyone born and raised in Baneford, so I thought of you."

"Thank you, Ed. That's very kind of you."

"Want to meet them?" he asked casually.

"The mayor?" she said, stunned.

"And the developer, too. Tomorrow. They're having a meeting at Dyeworks. I think you should come."

"I'd be honored."

Evelyn took a few seconds to register what Ed was saying. The old mill buildings at the west end of Main Street were colossal eyesores and a blight in the town, sorely in need of cleanup and renovation. At one point, over a century ago, Dyeworks alone, the biggest of the industrial buildings, employed almost half the town's residents. Back then, the factories meant something. They were monuments of pride, representing the strength of local industry. Today, the structures sat vacant and defaced, slowly collapsing over time.

In other, more desirable Massachusetts towns, developers were quick to purchase old mill buildings and repurpose them into offices and residential complexes, revitalizing old-world architecture *and* turning huge profits. High vaulted ceilings and brick façades were too costly to build with the current price of materials. Therefore, builders coveted certain types of older structures for their unique construction and historical appeal. Somehow, Baneford never made it into the development wave. It was a little too far north and perhaps just too unimportant for the developers to be interested. For that reason, the town's old mill buildings remained untouched while neighboring downtown areas received massive facelifts, gained new infrastructure, and earned vital tax revenue.

As an agent and lifelong resident, Evelyn only dreamed of being able to transform Baneford. The idea of facilitating a development of this size in whatever way she could made her skin tingle.

"I'd love to come, Ed."

"Great! I've heard you're the best real estate agent in Baneford. You *should* be there, and I'm glad to be the one to introduce you. We'll be standing outside at 10AM."

With that, Ed finished his coffee and left.

"What was that all about?" Trevor asked, turning in his seat.

"That was Officer Ed Crowley. We went to school together. He invited me to a developer meeting tomorrow."

"Nice. I wish I had more friends like that."

Evelyn spent some time at her desk imagining what Baneford would be like with the right urban planning. *Why not here?* she thought to herself. New offices attract big employers and create jobs. Tax dollars go toward bettering the roads and public schools. Perhaps eventually, savvy entrepreneurs would come too, opening restaurants, nightclubs, and fancy art galleries, in hopes of being part of the next big thing. With a few right ingredients and some luck, Baneford had the potential to get back on the map with the anticipated influx of social and economic activity.

Floating in her daydream, Evelyn didn't realize that the phone going off in the room was her own.

"Hello, this is Evelyn with EM Realty," she answered on the third ring, jolting herself back to reality.

"Hey, it's Sam."

"I'm sorry. Sam, who?"

"You don't recognize my voice, Evelyn? It's Sam...with Pondside Properties."

She realized this was Sam Burns, another old classmate, a fellow real estate agent, and, most irritatingly, a person she casually disliked. *Not this idiot*, she thought. The last time she'd seen Sam was at her open house when he'd rudely trotted his clients around, asking annoying questions with a smug expression on his face.

"How can I help you, Sam?"

"I have a client who wants to see your listing on Mox Street. Broker remarks state it's by appointment only. So, can you show it tonight?"

Evelyn didn't want to show it, and she certainly didn't want to see Sam, but Ed's praise still echoed in her ears, "The best real estate agent in Baneford." *Maybe his client will buy it, and I'll just be done with it.*

"Yes, I can show it. Does seven this evening work for you?"

"Seven works. See you there."

Sam hung up, and immediately, Evelyn's shoulders hunched forward. She didn't want to show the apartment but knew she had to. *It's the right thing to do*, she said to herself as she packed her things. If she left the office now, she'd get an hour's reprieve at home before Sam and his client came knocking.

In her apartment, she had just enough time for a quick meal and thirty minutes of sitting down with her book before she got herself ready to head downstairs and wait for Sam and his client to arrive. She saw a white mustang turn the corner onto Mox Street and pull up to the curb. Sam emerged from the car by himself, wearing a black leather jacket over a white t-shirt and jeans—an aggressive but failing attempt at looking cool.

"Who does this clown think he is?" she muttered under her breath.

"Hi, Evelyn. Thanks for meeting me here. My client will be here any minute," Sam said, stopping at the front steps.

"Of course."

"Actually, I think that's him now."

They watched a black limousine slowly descend the hill until it came to a stop in the middle of the street in front of the building. A well-dressed driver exited the car and walked around to the rear passenger side to open the door. Out stepped a suave man in a charcoal pinstripe suit.

"Hi, Grant," Sam said. Grant was tall, perfectly proportioned, clean-shaven, with neatly combed salt and pepper hair. His eyes were the same color as his tie, galaxy blue, and his tan remarkably even.

"Hi, Sam. Thanks for meeting me here. And who might you be? The listing agent?"

"Yes. I'm Evelyn May."

"Grant Blackwell. Pleasure to meet you," he said, gently taking her hand. "So, this is it?" Grant asked, looking at the building, then up and down the street. "Cute."

"Evelyn," Sam interjected, "can you tell us about the building before we head upstairs?"

"Yes. This is a two-story brownstone, one apartment on each floor. It was built in 1910. Both owners informally manage the association, sharing basic expenses down the middle, master insurance, repairs, and snow removal. Each unit has an individual water heater and gas furnace. The roof was redone about six years ago. The units don't have designated parking spots, but there's plenty of street parking, as you can see."

"Why is the owner selling?" Sam asked.

"She passed. Her son lives out of state, so he decided to put it on the market."

Grant nodded his head repeatedly, acknowledging everything she said, but refrained from asking any questions just yet.

"If you have any other questions, I'll be happy to answer them upstairs," she added.

They proceeded upstairs, past her own apartment, to the late Mrs. White's door.

Evelyn went room to room, flicking on the lights. She'd left a few pieces of furniture in the apartment for pseudo-staging, but all of Mrs. White's other belongings had gone to storage. Still, even with the few pieces inside, it showed like an old woman's apartment.

"As you can see, it's a three-bedroom, one-bath apartment, about fourteen hundred square feet. It needs some updating, and it's priced accordingly," Evelyn said, certain Sam's client would have no interest in buying the apartment.

Grant and Sam walked room to room without saying a word, then came back to meet Evelyn by the front door. "What do you think this would rent for?" Grant asked.

"I'm sure your agent can tell you what market rate is in Baneford," she replied, putting Sam on the spot. Sam attempted to formulate a response, but Evelyn cut him off immediately, asking Grant a question of her own. "I take it you're not looking to occupy; this would be an investment?"

"Correct. I'm going to be doing some business up here in Baneford, so I thought I'd check out the local inventory."

"And what do you think?"

"Evelyn, why don't you let me talk to my client, and we'll get back—" Sam started, trying to regain status in the conversation.

"It's not for me," Grant interrupted. "Let's not waste this nice woman's time."

Sam looked down at his feet, attempting to hide his disappointment.

"You might want to check out the area by Old Bedford. South of Main. I think you'll find more of what you're looking for," Evelyn said.

"I appreciate the tip, Evelyn," Grant replied, looking deeply into her eyes.

When they were done, she escorted them back downstairs where Grant's chauffeur stood waiting.

"Again, I appreciate your time," Grant said.

"My pleasure."

"By the way, who lives downstairs?" he asked, stepping into the back seat.

"Actually, I do."

"In that case, I might have to reconsider," Grant said, smiling, before closing the door.

Evelyn and Sam watched the limousine drive away, disappearing back over the top of the hill.

CHAPTER 2

THE TWO MEN sat in the open courtyard, watching the darkened sky, waiting for the courier to arrive. A brilliant display of stars twinkled overhead in the black. Adrian and Maruf felt an affinity for the stars because they, too, observed humanity from an uncommon position, distant from the frivolity of everyday life.

"Distance provides us with perspective," Maruf said, his eyes shining brightly.

"Then how come I still don't know what to do?" Adrian asked.

Maruf threw more wood on the fire, and it roared, sending a wave of heat over their bent knees. They'd spent many evenings here together, seated around the fire, recounting ghostly tales, sharing the wisdom of lonely men.

"Does man create the path? Or does the path lead the man?" Maruf asked.

"The man and the path can both go to hell," Adrian said, standing up and pacing anxiously in the courtyard.

Perched atop a hill, Maruf's home overlooked the banks of the Nile. Tall mudbrick walls painted white in Nubian style encircled the courtyard, separating the inner seating area from the outside. Peering over the edge of the wall, Adrian spotted a lone traveler walking through the tall grass.

"I think your man has come," he said.

A few minutes later, Mustafa, Maruf's trusted aide, appeared through the archway and took a seat with them by the fire. A light coat of sweat glistened on his brow, catching a few strands of his curly black hair, matting them down. He lit a cigarette and inhaled deeply.

"It's true. The young woman is cursed," he said, exhaling through his nose, letting the smoke travel over his mustache before curling up into the night air. Tall and slender, with dark skin, Mustafa resembled a spider when he sat before them, his knees bent in front of his chest, almost the same height as his shoulders.

"What did you see?" Maruf asked.

"They have her in chains around her wrists and ankles, fastened to a concrete wall, like an animal. Her own father keeps her this way. When she speaks, it is not the voice of a woman, and she is too strong."

"What do you mean?"

"They told me that she killed a man. Snapped his neck with her hands," he said, taking another drag. "I saw her pull the chains and break a piece of the wall. The strongest man could not do this."

Maruf threw another log on the fire and sat back, running his fingers through his beard. "Is that all?"

"They gave me this. They said she spit it from her mouth. They do not know where it came from." Mustafa dug his big hand into his pocket and took out a small white stone, not much larger than a copper coin. He tossed it over to Maruf, who held it in front of the fire, studying its detail.

"Perhaps our friend can tell us what this is," Maruf said, tossing the stone to Adrian.

Adrian also examined it carefully, looking at the markings on its side. "I do not know what this is, but it looks Egyptian."

"Do you see the bird at the top?" Maruf asked. "That is the god Horus. The box he stands on is called a serekh. Inside, a name is written. The name Djet."

"Who is that?"

"He was Egypt's pharaoh. One of the first kings, almost 5,000 years ago."

"Why did this woman spit a stone from her mouth with a pharaoh's name inscribed on it?" Adrian asked.

"If you care to help this woman, to help me do the work, *you* must tell me this."

"Jinns are your area of expertise, not mine."

"Jinns do not carry worldly items with them; they are not like the dead."

Adrian rolled the stone around in his hand and felt its smooth edges under his fingertips. He knew what Maruf wanted. Each of them had their abilities, and this was his.

"The woman Mustafa described is not dead," Adrian responded. "This item came to her somehow so that she could spit it from her mouth. I suspect the one who brought it to her is no longer alive."

Mustafa sat witnessing the exchange, a bit tired and hunched over from travel but eager nonetheless to see how they would devise a plan.

Adrian closed his fist over the stone and nodded his head. In recent years, he'd grown weary from using his gift. He'd used it ever since he was a boy trailing behind his mother, Nadia, in the Romanian countryside. Back then, communing with the dead filled him with wonder. He saw his ability as a special gift that very few receive. He came to learn that most souls lingering on the earth do not mean harm to the living but are merely trapped under the weight of a terrible sadness. He and his mother could see them, acknowledge their pain, and thereby set them free. *It is a great responsibility*, he used to think to himself.

As the years passed, however, he came to view his gift as more of a curse. A terrible burden. For every soul he set free, two more called to him, whispering their pain in his ear. When he slept, they entered his dreams like burglars in the night. He could not ignore them because their voices grew louder when he didn't stop to listen. If he chose to live a normal life, their calls would become deafeningly loud, almost maddening. Worst of all, he was bound to go where they summoned him. No matter how many souls he set free, he could not remain in a single place because the others gave him no mercy.

"Let me see," Adrian whispered, leaving the courtyard.

He descended the hill and walked through the tall grass toward the Nile. Reaching the water, he sat down on a bed of dried palm branches that formed a carpet over the moist ground. With the artifact in his hand, Adrian closed his eyes

26

and reached back in time. As if spying through a keyhole, he saw an unfamiliar place come into focus, a distant room in the long-forgotten past.

In a funerary complex constructed of granite and limestone, high priests in white linen hovered over a sarcophagus, their bald heads reflecting the light from the torches all around them. Carved into the sand-colored walls, floor-to-ceiling hieroglyphs sang the glory of the gods and exalted their pharaoh. The priests chanted in low octaves, reciting spells, as they pulled brain matter from the dead king's nostrils, placed his organs in canopic jars, and washed the inside of his hollowed abdomen with spiced wine.

On the periphery, subordinate priests observed the ritual preparation, tightly grasping the slender arms of the pharaoh's servants. Three men and two women, all with wild black hair darker than night, waited their turn. One by one, they tilted their heads back, pointing their gaunt, sorrowful faces at the ceiling as the priests poured poison from alabaster flasks into their mouths. They, too, would be entombed, a sacred obligation to serve their king in the afterlife.

The last servant to take the poison, a broad-shouldered young man, jerked his body violently, resisting the drink. He pushed them away, swinging his arms, shouting, "My wife and son, I cannot leave them!" It took four of them to subdue him. They held him by his shoulders, one arm around his narrow waist, and pulled his head back by its hair so strongly that the cartilage of his neck nearly snapped. When the young man shouted again, the poison quickly went into his mouth, and a hand went over his nose, forcing him to swallow. The pharaoh would have his servants in the afterlife. Before the life had left his body completely, they wrapped him in salt and linen, placing him in a sarcophagus of his own, along with a small white stone bearing the pharaoh's name, Djet, to whom the young man would forever belong.

Adrian opened his eyes, fixed them on the flowing water of the Nile, and waited for the anger in his heart to fade. He felt the young man's sorrow, the longing for his wife and son. Such immense pain had the power to transmute one's soul, allowing it to linger unnaturally in this world. Rolling the artifact in his fingers again, Adrian knew it was the same one placed in the box, carried by the young man's soul through the ages.

When he returned to the courtyard, he found Maruf and Mustafa spread across the floor, asleep by the dying fire. He took the same position, stretching his long legs over the quilted rug, and stared straight up at the stars. He wondered if he'd ever see her again. If he didn't, he wondered if she'd be proud of him, if she knew the things he did for the souls of strangers.

When the blinding hot sun appeared overhead, Adrian informed Maruf of his vision, leaving no detail unsaid. Shortly thereafter, Maruf conferred with Mustafa to send a message to the afflicted family. By late morning, they received word that their presence was requested.

"Will you travel with me?" Maruf asked Adrian.

"Why?"

"We will free the woman from possession, and it is best to do the work in the place you described. I will need your help."

"I do not know where that was," Adrian said. "I merely saw it."

"The place you described is in the desert near Souhag, where the ancient city of Abydos once stood," Maruf said. He lit a cigarette and disappeared into one of the rooms off the courtyard, leaving Adrian standing alone. When he returned a short while later, he wore a new white thobe with matching headdress like the desert Arabs wore.

"How long is the trip, and when will we return?" Adrian asked.

"It is a long drive, and we will return when God allows, inshallah," Maruf said, smiling through large, shining white teeth.

They met Mustafa outside the courtyard and walked with him along the banks of the Nile to the place they knew. There at the shore, Mustafa waived to the Nubian boatsman who would ferry them to Aswan. They sailed through calm waters with the wind at their back and arrived in Aswan at midday.

The boat docked, and they found themselves pushing past crowds of villagers at the pier, trying to get to Mustafa's rusted yet faithful Fiat sedan. Once in the vehicle, they traveled straight through the desert on a narrow two-lane road. Adrian sat in the back seat, quietly taking in the passing landscapes. Maruf and Mustafa smoked their cigarettes in the front of the car and enjoyed the melodies of old Arabic songs on the radio. With the windows rolled down, sand, smoke, and hot wind caressed their faces in an inconsistent rhythm, distorting their perception of the passing time.

"There it is," Maruf said eventually, pointing straight through the windshield at an ancient stone structure rising from the sand.

Mustafa went off the paved road and drove down a gravelly path in the sand toward the towering granite and limestone blocks. Adrian observed the funerary complex of Abydos and remembered his vision. The megalithic structure from before now appeared as crumbling ruins lost to time, but he recognized the shape of the rounded columns immediately. This was the place the servant was sacrificed for his pharaoh.

Off the beaten path, no tourists or security guards occupied the complex. Unlike more popular ancient sites in Egypt, this one remained isolated in the desert and open to anyone seeking to study its ancient past. Adrian did not see any other cars anywhere near the site. Maruf and Mustafa kindled a small fire on the ground outside the complex walls and hung a kettle over the flames to make the tea.

As the orange-yellow sun began to dip beneath the horizon, two vehicles appeared on the distant road and proceeded down the gravel path. The first car, a silver S600 Mercedes Benz, pulled up, followed by a ragged Toyota pickup truck hauling a large metal container on wheels behind it.

"They are a wealthy Egyptian family," Maruf whispered to Adrian. "This work will not go unrewarded."

The driver's side door of the Mercedes opened first, and an Egyptian man wearing a sport blazer and aviator sunglasses stepped out. He had a full head of short black hair, a dark complexion, and the barrel chest of an army general. A woman exited the passenger side, dressed in black robes with a veil wrapped loosely over her hair.

Maruf motioned for Adrian to join him as he went toward them. The man in the blazer took a few steps forward while his wife remained by the car.

"As-salamu alaykum, Mr. Naguib," Maruf said first and extended his hand.

"Wa-alaikum-salaam," the man said back, removing his glasses and taking Maruf's hand. "Who is this?" he asked, referring to Adrian.

"He is here to help me."

"He does not look Egyptian."

"He is very much not Egyptian," Maruf laughed, friendly in his tone.

Almost half a foot taller than both of them, Adrian's height and broad shoulders made him stand out in most places. Though his dark hair and olive skin suggested a multitude of possible backgrounds, Egyptian was not one of them. Now, he stood awkwardly, brooding and imposing, listening to them talk about him as if he were not there.

"Can you help?" Mr. Naguib asked.

"Let us see her," Maruf replied.

The man turned back to the Toyota truck and banged loudly on the hood. A thin driver in his fifties jumped out.

"Open it!" Mr. Naguib commanded.

The driver went around to the back of the truck to access the twenty-foot mobile container they'd hauled through the desert. He removed the padlock and pulled on the door, letting it swing open on its hinge, then hurriedly stepped away, allowing Maruf and Adrian to gaze inside. With daylight now gone, the inside of the box was pitch black. Mr. Naguib shined a flashlight in, allowing them to see her.

Like an animal, crouched on all fours, she sat squarely in the middle of the container, staring out with venom in her eyes. Her dark brown hair was long, knotted, and untamed, falling over her shoulders to her feet like a waterfall of dirty ribbons. Other than the chains fastened around her wrists and ankles, and the steel collar around her neck, she was completely naked in the metal box.

"Please," Mr. Naguib implored, his eyes downcast. "Help her."

"We must take her inside," Maruf said, pointing at what remained of the funerary complex.

The driver swiftly handed Adrian a key to unlock her chains before taking several large strides back. When they stepped into the container, she hissed at them like a stalking mountain lion. They could barely see inside, with their backs blocking the light. On his knees, Adrian fumbled in the dark to find the lock, and Maruf slowly drew closer to her, hunched over to keep his head from banging the ceiling.

"I found it," Adrian said. He unfastened a set of chains from their fixture on the ground, gently laying the loose end down.

"The one around her neck connects above," Mr. Naguib shouted into the box.

"Give me the key," Maruf said, extending his hand out in the dark.

With the key in his hand, Maruf crawled forward until his face came within inches of hers, close enough to feel her breath on his skin and see two eyes staring out from within the shadows.

"You are with her," Adrian warned.

Finding the fixture about his head, Maruf detached the chain and carefully put the loose end down. With the chains fastened to her hands, feet, and neck, no longer tethered to the container, she was free to move about and lunged forward at once, tackling Maruf onto his back, landing with her knees on his chest, breasts swinging over his face. When she groaned, they heard a voice that did not belong to a young woman but an old man with razor blades in his throat, bellowing in pain.

She shrieked and scratched at Maruf's head with her hands, trying to rip the flesh from his cheekbones. Her nails cut him, and he recoiled, bringing his elbows in and over his face to protect his eyes from being gouged out. Limited in movement by the confined space, Adrian came at her from the side, wrapping his long arm around her waist to pull her back. Unyielding, she squirmed in his grasp and wrestled her way free. He felt the coarse hair of her pelvis brush over his forearm before she slipped through his hold and crawled over Maruf's body, flinging herself from the container onto the yellow sand outside.

Stepping out from the container and seeing her in the light, Adrian and Maruf knew the spirit possessing her was a powerful one. Her skin looked deathly, pale, and gray. Rising to her feet, she growled at them with a deep and thunderous voice, strings of saliva dripping from her mouth. Her eyes rolled back into her head, yet they could still sense her staring, then she charged at them with all her strength.

They braced for the collision, but the chain around her neck tightened as she reached them. The tug from the taut chain yanked her body back violently, nearly tearing her head off.

Standing beside the container, Mr. Naguib held the other end of the chain in his hands, pulling his possessed daughter back. He shouted to them, "Hold her!"

Seeing their opportunity, Adrian leaped forward and grabbed one of her arms, Maruf the other.

"Mustafa!" Maruf shouted. "We need you."

Mustafa quickly found the chains to her hands and feet. When he pulled on them, her body jerked toward him, but Mr. Naguib pulled on his chain, yanking her back. If not for the otherworldly power in her body, this jostling could have torn her apart, yet she continued to resist.

They inched towards the complex, Mustafa and Mr. Naguib holding her chains, Maruf and Adrian clutching her shoulders tightly. When they reached the entrance of the crumbling structure, Mr. Naguib's wife came forward too, weeping for her daughter, her tears mixing with the mascara under her eyes, painting black lines down her face.

"Bring her here," Maruf said, guiding them to a few of the granite blocks that had collapsed out of the complex walls, conveniently landing side by side. "Place her over them."

Working together, they forced the daughter onto the granite slabs, using the chains to stretch her body over them like an animal on a butcher's block. Mustafa pulled her hands and feet toward him, her father pulled on her neck in the opposite direction.

"Keep her there!" Maruf shouted. He placed his hand on her forehead and spoke over her, alternating rapidly between Arabic and Nubian dialects; the others could not understand his meaning. When the young woman heard his voice, however, she cursed back at him loudly in a deep masculine octave.

"I am not your servant. You are a false god!" she proclaimed. Maruf placed his other hand down on her chest, pushing down just above her breasts, and continued with his incantation.

"You priests are filth! A scourge on the earth!" The woman groaned, her powerful, haunting voice echoing through the complex like thunder.

Adrian saw the desperation and fear in her parents' eyes. Mr. Naguib continued to hold the chains tightly, allowing the tears to roll down his face. At the other end of the blocks, Adrian observed Mustafa's forearm twitching under the stress, barely able to hold the chains any longer, losing the battle to the power in her hands and feet alone.

Maruf's voice grew louder as he repeated the incantations, rushing to draw the spirit out from its unwilling vessel. She convulsed under his palms, her nakedness wriggling in the moonlight; it was distressing to behold.

"He needs to remember now!" Maruf shouted to Adrian, inviting him to use his gift.

Adrian stepped closer to stand across from Maruf and hovered over the woman. He breathed deeply, calming his mind, preparing himself for the task at hand. He gazed down into the woman's eyes, looking deep within them. Adrian imagined himself melting into them like butter in a hot pan. As he dipped below the surface, a memory came rushing forward—of a man taken from his family many millennia ago.

A young man from the desert stood with his wife and young son. He watched the dunes, waiting for the men to come. The faint glow of torches in the distance grew brighter until the priests were all around them. "Your service to the pharaoh is not complete," they said, grabbing him by the arm. The bald-headed priests led his body back to the pharaoh, but his eyes stayed on his wife and son, memorizing the shape of their silhouettes against the desert sand until they became too small to see.

"I see him!" Maruf exclaimed.

Occupying the same space as the young woman, Adrian and Maruf saw the outline of a man's body, translucent in form, shining with a soft blue light. Adrian removed the white stone from his pocket and held it over the woman's face, but it was the young man inside who recognized what it was.

"Djet is not your pharaoh. You serve him no longer."

Hearing the words, the woman bellowed out in despair, a masculine cry, and Adrian felt the young man's pain.

"This is not your vessel. You will be reunited with your wife and son, so you must not keep this woman from her family, as we will not keep you from yours," Adrian continued.

The blue light shined brightly, and they glimpsed a look of peace on the young man's face. It was only for a moment before he floated away from her, disappearing into the night air, and her convulsions stopped.

Mr. Naguib and his wife watched, bewildered, until they saw the color of their daughter's skin change back to its normal appearance, warm, familiar flesh. Their daughter lay perfectly still across the stones as if in a deep and peaceful sleep. Mr. Naguib removed the chains from her body, and they clinked and rattled one last time as he cast them aside, falling to the ancient sand. Mr. and Mrs. Naguib embraced their daughter, and tears of joy streamed from their eyes.

They happily led their daughter to the car and placed her in the backseat. Mr. Naguib returned with a black leather carry bag, which he handed to Maruf. "I am eternally grateful," he said, bowing his head before turning back toward the car.

The Mercedes left first, and the truck followed, hauling the empty metal container away. When they were out of sight, Maruf opened the bag and showed Adrian. Inside were countless stacks of Egyptian bills, packed densely.

"What is this?" Adrian asked.

"The fee you earned," Maruf replied. "The man whose daughter you helped is very wealthy. This is his gratitude. Half is yours."

Immediately, Adrian thought of Evelyn. In the past, receiving or letting go of money never carried much weight to Adrian because he knew the voices of the dead found him anywhere, across any distance, and currency held no power there. With more than enough money to travel and stay with her now, Adrian struggled to put the thought out of his mind. *You would only go to leave again*, he lamented to himself. He left without saying goodbye because it was never meant to be. But a life with Evelyn is what Adrian wanted most.

For the next few days, they stayed in Maruf's village home, and people came to visit with him. They sat before him in the open courtyard in the fresh air, asking for his protection, one family after the other. Often, what they really wished was for Maruf to bring them good fortune, but that's not what those who hear the dead do. He was a medium, just like Adrian, unburdened by curses and particularly skilled at confronting evil sown in ancient times. Still, Maruf entertained his guests and performed symbolic rituals to give his village a sense of peace.

Adrian understood that Maruf considered these sessions a formality, serving no real practical purpose. He watched it all from a distance, sitting alone at the other end of the courtyard. The people who came were not haunted or vexed, merely superstitious, seeking any means of protection against the perils of the world.

At night, when the Nubian women drummed and chanted in front of the fire, Adrian heard beauty in the songs. He decided the ceremonies weren't so impractical after all because the ability to evoke profound emotion, he knew, had the power to heal broken souls. The women's rhythms were hypnotic and seductive, their chanting candid and raw. With torches burning in the desert air and music penetrating the hearts of those gathered, the ceremonies were invigorating like cool winds at the end of a hot day under the sun.

The melodies lulled him to sleep, and Adrian saw her in his dreams. Evelyn walked past a white clock tower and entered a wide dark hall with menacing figures lurking in the shadows. Malevolent energy whirled around her like a swarm of locusts. The figures in the shadows bowed to one among them who summoned a darkness from underneath the ground. Adrian saw the darkness as a hole opening in the earth, ready to swallow the world. The figures brought their fellows forward and tossed them into the depths, feeding the darkness. He heard tearing and gnawing sounds, the mastication of raw flesh.

Supernatural forces surrounded whatever structure he saw Evelyn enter; he did not perceive one spirit but many. A collective consciousness of souls. Adrian sensed their awful intention and knew she would be in danger. Early the next morning, Maruf found Adrian already awake, looking out over the twilight landscape, with a packed bag resting at his feet.

"The time has come for me to leave," Adrian said.

"May you travel safely and return with peace upon you."

CHAPTER 3

EVELYN AWOKE TO the melodious chirping of birds outside her bedroom window. On this morning, they sang of hope and the potential of what could be. Instead of her typical morning ritual of groggily pressing snooze several times, Evelyn got out of bed enthusiastically before the alarm sounded. Seated on a stool in her kitchen with a steaming cup of coffee in hand, she watched the day's first light bring color to the world. In her head, she thought of things she would say at the meeting about herself, about real estate, and the town. She didn't know what their topics of discussion would be, but the idea of playing a role, however small, in shaping Baneford's future sent currents of elation down her spine. She imagined walking her late parents down the street, pointing at the contributions she'd made. When Evelyn went for the next sip of coffee and found her mug empty, she realized how far into the daydream she'd gone.

She sprang from the stool to get ready, knowing that in a few short hours, she'd be seated with the mayor and a prestigious real estate developer. Evelyn carefully curated her outfit for the meeting, opting to wear her black heels and two-piece pantsuit. Given that the gathering was set inside the abandoned tannery, which residents simply referred to as "Dyeworks," Evelyn questioned whether heels were the practical choice as she rushed out the door. But when all heads on the street turned as she passed by, her worries disappeared.

She arrived at the west end of Main Street several minutes ahead of schedule, with spare time to admire the exterior of the old tannery. Set apart from the nearby residential neighborhoods, Dyeworks sat in the industrial district, along with a handful of the town's old mill buildings. Abutting the tannery and directly across the street, two other factories also crumbled away in this abandoned stretch of the city. Behind the tannery, a small bend of the Washisund River straddled the property line, then ran north, snaking through a heavily wooded area.

Dyeworks was the largest and most architecturally impressive structure on the street. Rising three stories high—tall by old-world town standards—the building's brick façade inspired quiet awe, while the white clock tower floating over the roofline boasted of its singularity. White stone arches adorned the front entrance and loading docks, protruding over the red brick, offering a touch of regality. Unusual for factories this size, the building's roof was not flat but pitched, assembled with tiny black shingles, pointing up at the sky. Underneath, dozens of black-trimmed windows lining the entire width of the exterior provided a stark contrast against the red brick.

Evelyn breathed in the refreshing spring air and admired the masonry, trying to imagine how Dyeworks must have appeared in its heyday. She tried to see past the brick face that needed repainting, the warped sections of roof, the haphazard graffiti strewn here and there, and the massive cracks running through the pavement like varicose veins. *This is going to be a massive project*, Evelyn said to herself. Even the neighborhood, once the seat of serious economic activity, now housed a homeless and drug-addicted population, adding to residents' concerns.

With more square footage than any other building in Baneford, whatever the developers chose to do, the project would surely benefit the town. Standing beside the main door, visibly sealed, she waited patiently for the others to arrive.

"Evelyn!" Ed called out. Dressed in his police blues, Ed stood in a second, smaller doorway beneath the clock tower, motioning for her to join him.

"I didn't know you were here already," she said. "I was just admiring Dyeworks from the outside."

"Wait till you see the inside," he replied. "Come, they're all here."

When they passed through the door, Evelyn was immediately struck by the enormity of the building's inner hall. An entirely separate two-story structure could fit inside the ground floor, with plenty of room left over on all sides, including above. The factory floor ran the full width of the building, with high, scaffolded ceilings above.

All the old tanning drums, each one standing at least twelve feet high, were positioned in pairs, running down the center of the hall. Evelyn recalled from school history lessons that these were the containers tanneries used for their manufacturing process, first filling them with all sorts of hides and dyes, then turning the drums over and over by hand until saturation. Vertical support columns ran parallel to the drums, spanning the same distance across the factory, with sunlight from the windows hitting the columns, projecting slender striped shadows everywhere. A century of dust covered the floor, mixed with the litter of old leather, machine bits, and paper. *A snapshot of the past*, Evelyn thought to herself.

The upper level consisted entirely of partitioned offices, circling the factory from above like balcony seats at a sports arena. It was an unusual addition given the sometimes-unpleasant fumes emanating from below, but the Dyeworks owners had keen eyes for watching their lucrative production line. With broken windows and doors hanging off their hinges, the offices no longer reflected the prestigiousness the executives who occupied them at one point surely felt. Peering left and right and up through the scaffolding, Evelyn visualized luxury apartments replacing the empty space around her.

"They're over here," Ed said, leading her to the other end of the building.

As they drew closer, Evelyn saw several businessmen and women on the other side of the drums, seated around a long table brought in for the occasion.

They looked up when Evelyn and Ed entered. To her surprise, Grant Blackwell was among those seated. She stopped several feet away and smiled in friendly greeting, awaiting her invitation to sit. Meanwhile, Ed went forward to the head of the table and whispered in the mayor's ear. At once, Mayor Jenkins stood up and gestured for Evelyn to take one of the empty seats nearby.

"Please, join us!"

She circled the table to sit down, and Ed took the seat next to her.

"I'm grateful for all of you being here today," the mayor said. "Allow me to introduce everyone here local to Baneford, and then I'll ask that you kindly introduce yourselves again so that we remember your individual names."

"Wonderful," the sharply dressed woman at the other end of the table said, clapping her hands once. In her mid-forties, with long flowing black hair and lips painted a power red, it was clear she was the leader of their development group.

"As you all know, I'm Mayor Marty Jenkins, born and raised in Baneford. Throughout my term, I've committed to working with developers to bring new infrastructure to our town. We've decluttered many of our approval and zoning processes to make things faster and more financially appealing for our development partners. I consider projects like these a win-win. I'm joined on my right by Lieutenant Ed Crowley, recently appointed to oversee town safety and security."

Evelyn, never having seen the mayor speak in person, suddenly felt proud to be his constituent, sensing in him the right qualities of a leader. Though not impressive in stature, with small beady eyes and thinning brown hair, the mayor appeared big in his confidence and sounded sure in his cadence.

"And on my right," he continued, "Mr. Stewart Dinklage, deputy mayor of Baneford. Stewart has been my right-hand man for two years, and I'm sure you'll all get to know him well in due time."

Stewart shot a pained half-smile to the group. In complete contrast to his superior, Stewart was tall, wiry, and timid. He hid behind large glasses and fine blonde hair that fell over his brow, touching the tops of the frames.

"I've also asked one of our town's top real estate brokers to join us at this meeting," the mayor said, looking in Evelyn's direction. "Please, if you wouldn't mind introducing yourself."

Not expecting to address everyone so soon, her heart thudded heavily in her chest, and she felt the pressure change in her ears. Without time to think, Evelyn stood up from her seat and opened her mouth to speak, hoping the words that came would be the right ones. She noticed Grant perk up in his seat just as her lips began to move.

"Hello, everyone. My name is Evelyn May. I, too, was born and raised in Baneford. I manage a real estate brokerage down the street called EM Realty. Before that, I worked for a national real estate franchise I'm sure you've all heard of. Last year, we were the top firm in town by volume. I'm delighted to be here, honored to be in the good company of our mayor, and excited to hear what wonderful things might be coming."

The woman with long black hair at the far end of the table nodded in approval, and Grant smiled.

"Thank you, Evelyn. I'm glad you're here," the mayor said. "Miss Hyde, would you do us the honor of introducing your team?"

"Certainly, Mr. Mayor, and please, call me Ursula," she said, making sure to smile at everyone in the room. With light hazel eyes, she had a piercing gaze reminiscent of wild wolves. "My company, Hyde Properties, has been active in the acquisition and development of real estate for the past fifteen years," she said, making sure to smile at each person at the table. "We've successfully bought and sold over five hundred million dollars' worth of real estate during that time. We specialize in revitalizing dilapidated areas and underutilized assets along the northeast."

Ursula commanded the room with a tone that was gentle and laid back. She rattled off an impressive resume, but her self-assuredness came from a different place, and Evelyn sensed a unique power within her.

"We, too, are grateful for the opportunity to be in this wonderful town," she continued. "This building is exactly the type of asset we look for, but our sights are set on more than just one project here. As many of the municipalities we've developed in can tell you, the influx of revenue and commercial activity our projects bring has done wonders for their respective communities."

Seated next to Ursula, three of her staff nodded in agreement while Grant stared straight ahead, seemingly impatient, waiting for introductions to end.

"Of course, I am nothing without my team," she said in a humble tone but with a mischievous grin. "I'm joined by Mr. Terry Pincher," pointing at the fine-featured man seated across from Evelyn, "And Mr. Fred Isakov," a heavyset older man wearing a sweater vest under his suit jacket. "Both of whom are executive directors at my Hyde

Properties." Turning toward her only female associate, an attractive brunette with a tan complexion and intimidating cheekbones, she continued, "Miss. Analisa Gomez is head of public relations for Hyde Properties. And last but not least, Mr. Grant Blackwell here is not officially with my company, but he is our honored guest and financial partner, with whom we see a bright future ahead."

Evelyn realized that when Grant had said he was in town for business the previous night, he was referring to Dyeworks and his partnership with Ursula.

"Excellent, thank you," the mayor replied. "We're going to keep today's meeting relatively brief and to the point. I'd like to hear your company's vision for Baneford, and we'll offer some guidance as the local team on what we think can actually happen here, with Dyeworks being the first item on the agenda."

With all the introductions out of the way, Ursula presented her vision for Dyeworks. She proposed a mixed-use development, where sixty percent of the building's gross square footage would be earmarked for commercial development, the bulk of it as class-A office space on top and retail below. The remaining forty percent would be developed into residential apartments in two stacks, half for sale and half for rent. As she spoke, Ursula intermittently looked to Terry and Fred for numbers, which they mechanically rattled off, citing construction timelines, costs, and floorplan measurements.

Mayor Jenkins relied on Ed for his opinions on how the construction might affect the town from a logistics and transportation perspective, while Stewart cited local zoning laws and possible variances the mayor's office could push through for the project.

"Evelyn, based on your experience, do you think our town can absorb the residential component with nearly three hundred units available for sale and for rent?" the mayor asked.

Put on the spot again, Evelyn was more confident to speak this time because no one more than her habitually monitored the pulse of the local market.

"Many of our out-of-town buyers come to Baneford for the affordability but complain about the lack of employment options nearby. I would say the absorption would depend heavily on the office component of the project and which employers Miss. Hyde has in mind for commercial tenancy on this project and others down the line," she replied.

Ursula leaned forward, having listened intently. "My dear, that is a very intelligent remark and one that I'm happy to address. For the bulk of the office space, we're currently in talks with several large technology companies interested in transporting their headquarters here. We plan to build the office as a built-to-suit project, ensuring our commercial tenant is ready for migration the day after completion. Analisa is also keeping us apprised on that front."

Ursula's quick response pleased the mayor, and a discussion ensued. Ed addressed safety, the mayor and Stewart discussed revenue, while Ursula and Grant focused on timelines and costs. It was made clear that Hyde would preserve the architectural integrity of the front façade.

"I like what I'm hearing here, everyone," the mayor jumped in. "Let's schedule our next meeting in two weeks, and please have your preliminary designs ready. In tandem, we'll begin to speak with our zoning council and conservation committee to prep them for the legal work ahead."

"Nice job today," Ed said to Evelyn.

"Thank you for inviting me."

"Very nice to have you with us," Mayor Jenkins added.

Mayor Jenkins went forward to shake hands with his counterparts, leaving Evelyn and Ed standing alone. As they walked back through the hall together and exited through the door under the clock tower, Evelyn felt like she'd just emerged from the strangest dream.

"I'll let you know when the next one is. I'll see you soon," Ed said, walking to his car.

Evelyn turned to take in the sight of Dyeworks again and breathed a sigh of exhilaration before heading to her office. For the next two hours, her head remained in the clouds, floating above her colleagues, distant from their terrestrial chatter. Hiding at her desk, staring over the top of the screen at the street outside, Evelyn watched the pedestrians of her town stroll by and continued to dream.

In the midafternoon, Evelyn left the office to walk and clear her mind. However, she quickly realized that keeping her finely pointed heels from getting wedged in the sidewalk cracks would require serious focus. She walked with her eyes down, scanning to avoid the traps. Passing the town library, she looked up. It was where she'd first gotten to know Adrian, sitting with him, pouring over the books. Staring up at those two white pillars bordering the entrance now, a familiar feeling came into her heart. *Where are you?* she wondered.

Evelyn walked a bit further and thought to call Casey to share the news of the day with her. As she reached for her phone, she spotted Grant leisurely walking down the street, coming her way. Seeing her, he quickened his pace.

"Evelyn!" He waved enthusiastically.

"Hi, Grant."

"I don't typically believe in fate, but I'd say there's a good chance we were meant to meet. That's three times in two days," he said, maintaining eye contact.

"Maybe Baneford is just a small town," she bantered back.

"Anyway, I didn't realize the agent showing me the apartment last night was also the best agent in town and confidant to the mayor. I've clearly been speaking to the wrong people."

"I'm hardly all that," she said, blushing.

"I'd like you to have dinner with me," Grant asserted boldly, taking a half-step closer.

Evelyn looked into his cobalt blue eyes, searching for the right thing to say. He stared right back at her, cool and collected. Seeing her about to stammer, he followed up with a second question.

"Are you seeing anyone?"

"No," she replied, shaking her head.

"Do you have plans tonight?"

"I was just about to call my friend to make plans," Evelyn said, looking at her phone.

"Then you're free tonight," he said, smiling. "We won't stay out late. I'll pick you up at your place at seven."

Evelyn liked how clear and purposeful Grant was in his communication. She didn't have time to think about Adrian, who wasn't in Baneford anyway. *This man is rich, attractive, and charming*, she said to herself, *you're crazy if you don't agree*.

"Sure, why not. I look forward to it," she said finally.

"Great, I'll see you in a few hours."

Grant nodded to her and then continued walking, and she watched until he turned at the corner after the library. Evelyn hadn't been on a single date since Adrian left. She thought of him all the time but had no idea if he'd ever come back. Even with every right to go on this date, something felt off. *I need to let Adrian go*. That was the only thing left to do.

Evelyn managed to call Casey on her way home and promptly informed her that she'd be going out with a mysterious and wealthy businessman, likely fifteen years her senior. She wanted to say more, to tell her friend about the meeting at Dyeworks, too, but Evelyn felt she'd reached her friend at a bad time.

"Yeah? Good for you," Casey muttered back, not sounding even marginally interested.

"I have more things to tell you," Evelyn said. "That is... if you want to hear them."

Evelyn could hear the television playing loudly in the background. Judging by her friend's flat voice and the crinkling sound of fast-food wrappers, she guessed Casey was horizontally on the couch with some type of bingeable snack in her hands.

"Sure, call me later," Casey said, eager to return to her show. "We'll talk later."

Chalking it up to nothing more than a mood, Evelyn hung up and returned home with ample time to pick out another outfit for the evening, which she assumed would take place in some sort of fancy dining establishment. She put on her black cocktail dress and wrapped an elegant shawl over her shoulders, hoping her choice would be appropriate for the unknown destination.

At precisely seven in the evening, she heard a car pull up outside, followed by two short beeps of the horn. Grant's black limousine awaited her. The chauffeur promptly opened the backdoor, and she took her seat beside Grant, who welcomed her warmly. She noticed the subtle scent of his cologne, and the privacy wall inside the car, with the chauffeur on the other side.

"Thank you for joining me. You look stunning," he said, looking at her with admiration.

Evelyn didn't feel the way she often did when men hit on her—objectified and uncomfortable. Instead, she appreciated Grant's forward but respectful style of sophisticated flirtation. Inspiring a different reaction in her than Baneford men, Evelyn did not feel objectified or uncomfortable; instead, she felt valued and seen.

"Thank you for the invitation and for picking me up," she said warmly, hoping to make up for her earlier clumsy attitude.

"Oh, that's the least I can do. Plus, I know you've had a big day. You deserve a night off to just relax and have someone else take care of the plans."

"You had a big day, too," she laughed. "We were at the same meeting."

"Yes, but the mayor wasn't relying on me for expert real estate advice," Grant joked back.

"By the way, where are we going?" Evelyn asked, noticing the car turning north on the highway instead of south to Boston. She figured he'd be taking her downtown, though clearly, that wasn't the plan.

"A restaurant on the water. I have a feeling you'll love it. Don't worry. I'll have you back before bedtime," he said with a boyish smile.

At the Bella Luna Restaurant in Newbury Port, the maître d' guided them to their table. From the top of the cliff, the dining room overlooked the bay, and the table Grant reserved offered the best view in the house. Evelyn looked out over all the sailboats below, and a sense of calm came over her. She noticed the dim light, heard the jazz music playing softly in the background, and picked up the aroma of good food. A few glasses of wine later and a taste of the appetizer selection, she stopped feeling awkward and relaxed into the evening.

"Marty Jenkins seems like a pretty good partner for us; what do you think?" Grant said, and Evelyn believed in his sincerity in wanting her opinion.

"He seems genuinely interested in bringing new development to Baneford."

"We pick partners very selectively. Being pro-business can't be the only criteria, so we look for towns and officials who are dependable and dedicated."

"How long have you worked with Hyde Properties?" Evelyn asked.

"That's a good question. I'm not actually *with* Hyde Properties. We've done a few projects, and we have an effective arrangement. Basically, they find killer deals, and I bring most of the money to get the developments done," Grant said, shrugging his shoulders and smiling. "That's the simplest way to put it."

The waiter placed their entrees on the table, and Evelyn savored the taste of fresh pasta and properly paired wine.

"Where are you from?" she asked.

"All over at this point. But I've spent plenty of time in Massachusetts. My alma mater is here, so it's always been a familiar place."

Evelyn assumed Harvard. He looked like a man whose refinement began at an early age, making him well-educated, well-traveled, and wiser than his years. With his salt-and-pepper hair and handsome features, Grant seemed the quintessential gentleman, and she could not deny the appeal.

They talked for hours, and Grant shared more about himself with Evelyn than she thought he would. Much of the conversation centered around work, but she enjoyed hearing the details of how real estate development deals are structured and learning how people at the top thought about money.

"I'm an equity investor in Hyde Property deals, and I'm also a general partner overseeing the capital raising. My firm specializes in placing equity, essentially raising money for deals that offer outsized returns. Because I'm able to bring such large sums from our network of high-net-worth individuals and family offices, I receive ownership of the development company, sharing in the upside fees."

"Personally, I'm excited about how the development could transform the town," Evelyn said.

"Absolutely. I've seen new schools get built, new businesses open, and lots of low-income families benefit from the projects we've done. It is exciting for the towns."

"When I think about what it could be like, I imagine the town with better opportunities, a nicer downtown area, new shops and restaurants, and more sophisticated people coming from the city or internationally."

"Maybe you can give us some ideas since you're born and raised. Even big developments start as a few words, nothing more than a conversation. The next time we see each other, you'll tell me about your vision of downtown Baneford in more detail."

When the limousine returned them to Mox Street, Evelyn thanked Grant for a lovely evening. He exited the vehicle this time and walked around the car to open her door and plant a light kiss on her cheek.

"Pleasure was all mine," he said, waving goodbye.

The limousine took off before Evelyn could get inside her building, and for the final two hours of the evening, Evelyn lay in bed, reflecting on the day and how the potential for great things to happen loomed in sight. Professionally, she saw bigger ventures on the horizon, but personally, for the first time, Evelyn allowed herself to dream about the future. She was not the type to be enamored by wealth alone, but the universe took away Adrian and presented Grant. He wasn't just rich like Casey's parents, but wealthy at an entirely different level. It was the sort of life she could barely imagine.

Sure, he's older, Evelyn thought, *but he's also handsome, charming, and kind.* In terms of potential partners, it would be difficult, based on first dates only, to already have reasons for why Grant was not an ideal partner. *Because of Romanian necromancers*, she told herself.

CHAPTER 4

THINGS WERE RELATIVELY quiet the rest of the week as the excitement from the big meeting slowly faded away. Determined to lift Casey from her malaise, Evelyn forced her from the apartment early on Saturday morning for some fresh air. She arrived at her door with three heavy knocks, calling Casey to let her in. Nearly two minutes later, Casey came to the door looking disheveled in gray sweatpants and a ripped flannel shirt.

"Good morning," Evelyn said.

"Yeah, good to see you," Casey said, rubbing her eyes.

"You don't work on Saturdays anymore, right?"

"No, I haven't felt like training on the weekends."

"I know it's been hard, but I'm here because I want us to go out and for you to be the Casey I remember."

"I'll get there eventually," she said, shrugging her shoulders. "What do you want to do?"

Evelyn proposed a leisurely stroll outside to start the day. Casey took some time to get ready, changing, washing her face, and putting sneakers on. Evelyn followed her around the apartment, filling her in on recent news. She told Casey about the meeting with the mayor, Hyde Properties, and Grant. She was pleasantly surprised to see Casey's interest piqued at the town's possible redevelopment. Though Casey's family resided in Old Bedford now, she'd lived most of her life in Baneford and, like Evelyn, had always wished for the town to elevate in some way.

As children and adolescents, Evelyn and Casey fantasized about being in other places where worldly, sophisticated people lived. On other occasions, they fantasized about Baneford changing, becoming more than it was. They remembered those dreams as they walked through the familiar neighborhoods, taking in the sight of the budding maple trees in the sun, talking, and connecting as they'd always done. A cool but temperate breeze accompanied them on their stroll.

Hearing about Evelyn's date with Grant, Casey felt a twinge of jealousy that reminded her just how empty her life was at the moment. Struck with a sudden urge to crawl out of her funk, she held her posture a little straighter and projected her voice with more confidence the longer they walked. Evelyn noticed the subtle changes in her friend and was pleased. With the imminent shift of seasons, she hoped that Casey, too, could have her reawakening and thrive.

On the way back to the apartment, the conversation shifted to Casey's life, and Evelyn saw that the real progress would come slow. Casey did not have any recent romances, hobbies, interests, or stories to share. In fact, she'd done little of anything since the horrible events with Hendrick. Casey spoke of her family going on vacation, of clients moving on, of who she heard was getting married, but nothing of herself. Evelyn feared how long this depression could last.

Later in the evening, for a change in venue, and because Casey didn't have any fresh ingredients, they took a ride to

Evelyn's apartment to make dinner. There, they spent more hours talking in the dimly lit kitchen, drinking wine while preparing their meal as a peaceful energy filled the room. Something about being together in that apartment, a space they'd both known since childhood, felt wholesome and secure—it was an unspoken truth they shared.

After dinner, they retired to the living room and sank into the sofa, throwing their feet up on the coffee table.

"So, do you like him?" Casey asked.

"There's not a lot to dislike at this point."

"You're seeing him again?"

"I don't know if he's planning to ask me out again," Evelyn said earnestly.

Casey smirked at Evelyn's habitual aloofness with respect to how men saw her. Therefore, it was her great delight to subtly tell Evelyn each time it was relevant that nearly all men undoubtedly found her appealing.

"He'll ask you out. Trust me. He'll do it soon, too."

After a cozy night together, Evelyn made a bed for Casey on the couch. Evelyn flicked off the lights and proceeded to her bedroom to sleep. In the darkness, she watched her curtain sway from the light breeze coming through the window cracks. As it ebbed and flowed, Evelyn whispered prayers for Casey and Adrian, pleading for their safety and happiness. As she whispered the words, the emotion of almost losing them came rushing back, and tears collected at the corners of her eyes.

It was no light thing what Casey had gone through, nearly strangled to death, then witnessing the brutal murder of her boyfriend so soon after. It pained Evelyn to think about Adrian, how he'd sacrificed his life for her, only to leave town later without saying a word. She fell asleep wishing she had the power to reverse evil or let go of its memory. *If only we could forget the past.*

The next morning, Casey returned home, looking a bit more alive than when she had left. Evelyn spent that Sunday doing chores—groceries, cleaning, laundry—but her mind wandered throughout. She continued to think about Casey and Adrian, and a pervading urge to do something for them permeated her consciousness. *I don't know what it is,* she whispered in futility.

As the day came to an end, wishing to change the direction of her thoughts, Evelyn resumed reading where she'd left off, just about one-third of the way through Hurston Laurent's book. The familiar tone of the narration quickly put her at ease. Only half a chapter in, she was surprised to receive a phone call from an unknown number.

"Hello?" she answered timidly.

"Evelyn, this is Stewart from Mayor Jenkins' office. I'm sorry to bother you this late on a Sunday. Is there any chance you could pass by our office tomorrow? There's something the mayor would like to ask you."

"Sure, yes. I could be there at 1PM. Does that work, and is there anything I should know in advance?"

"That time works, and no, that won't be necessary. Again, sorry to call this late," he said, hanging up abruptly.

That was a strange way to schedule a meeting, she thought before returning to the book. Evelyn read for another hour before switching off her bedside lamp. Sleep came to her quickly that night because she'd expended all of her emotional energy worrying about things she could not control.

Close to the Old Bedford city limits, on a wide street lined with oak trees hundreds of years old, the mayor's office was in a two-story white neoclassical building with stately columns out front. Arriving outside the next day, Evelyn admired the American flag flying overhead. A smaller black flag flew underneath, commemorating those missing in action or taken prisoner in the country's wars. She walked in the entrance, her briefcase in hand, believing her actions to be likewise in service of her home.

A security guard handed Evelyn a lanyard and guided her to the guest elevator. It opened onto a reception room, set up as a lounge, with golden framed portraits hanging on the vaulted walls. They featured various prominent men from Baneford's history, stately with their gray hair, posing regally with their chins pointed at the heavens. She walked across the red carpet to the seating area and waited for some time before Stewart came to collect her.

"Thank you for coming," he said, walking and talking quickly.

Unlike how he'd appeared when she first saw him, timid and withdrawn, Stewart now seemed a bit frantic, propelled by some fantom energy that pushed him outside of his natural reticence.

"Please, come with me. We're glad you're here," he said, his cadence choppy and rushed.

Evelyn saw that he moved in a jerky way, and his mouth twitched slightly as if struggling to hold back words.

Scampering unnaturally, he led her across the reception hall toward the wooden doors that opened into the mayor's expansive office. Mayor Jenkins sat behind an enormous mahogany desk, the top of his balding head reflecting the light from his table lamp. There were dark circles under his eyes, and they were downcast as he read the documents on his desk. He did not look up when they entered, giving Evelyn time to survey the room.

One wall consisted entirely of wooden bookshelves, floor to ceiling, filled with leather-bound volumes with gold lettering. A glittering chandelier hung above at the center of the room. Beneath it, a formal Victorian seating area for tea or coffee complimented with period benches and chairs. At the other end of the room, wide bay windows overlooked the street below.

In the far corner, seated alone, Evelyn noticed Ed in his police blues, slouched over in a chair with its back to the room. He didn't appear to notice anyone coming in or out and sat motionless, staring out the window. Before she could say hello to Ed, Stewart insisted that Evelyn sit on the couch, then promptly scuttled over to whisper something in the mayor's ear. He kept his eyes fixed on Evelyn as he whispered.

"Evelyn!" the mayor announced suddenly, standing up. "Thank you for coming on such short notice."

"Of course. I'm happy to be here."

"Things have been moving very fast with the Hyde team, and we're pleased to say the project is going forward," the mayor explained, walking around his desk to stand in front of her.

"That's great news," she said.

The mayor's face was different from the first time she met him. He appeared older. Opposite from how he'd come across at the meeting, energetic and confident, he now came across vacant, stripped of his sympathy.

"We're very excited too, and we'd like to invite you to become a consultant on this project. We've heard good things from you, and we'll benefit from your insights."

"I am happy to be of help."

"We've approved preliminary plans, and Hyde Properties are currently acquiring Dyeworks, set to close tomorrow," the mayor said, breathing heavily, his chest heaving.

"I didn't realize it could be that fast. What about environmental?"

"They'll be doing it post-close. Special circumstances for this one," he said, with defensiveness in his tone.

Though she was a residential agent, she understood that commercial properties, especially old factories, required clean phase one and two environmental test results before a sale, should remediation be required. She'd never heard of belaying contamination risk and wondered if it was unique to this deal or common practice in larger commercial deals.

"Understood," she said, fearing to speak up and sound dumb.

"What we'd appreciate right now are your opinions on the potential sales and rental income from the residential component of the project."

"Sure, I can work on it this afternoon."

The mayor nodded his head to signal the meeting was over and went back to his desk immediately, diving back into his documents. Evelyn sensed in him a desperation, and despite the good news, he seemed aggravated and distracted. Before turning to leave, Evelyn shot a look over to Ed, who remained seated with his back to the room, in a trance.

At the top of the stairs, Stewart greeted her awkwardly and then pushed a dossier into her hands.

"Those are some notes on what we're looking for," he said, gritting his teeth.

"Got it."

Walking back through the grand entrance of the building onto the street, Evelyn came away not knowing what to think. *Why are they so agitated?* she asked herself. The interaction gave her a strange feeling, but she decided to dive into the work right away because this had the potential to be a pivotal moment for the town and for her career. *I'm going to kill it on this project, no matter how strange they're acting,* she decided.

Evelyn spent all the afternoon and evening hours researching and typing feverishly on her computer. She pulled real estate data from Baneford and surrounding towns and analyzed it carefully, looking at unit sizes, amenity packages, building designs, rental rates, and sales comparables. Once she'd sorted the information into tables, Evelyn drew her conclusions from the data and began writing the summary of her findings. In her report, she presented the revenue projections broken down by category in one section, then added personal notes in a second section, detailing additional ways a revitalization of the area could benefit the town.

Baneford's homeless occupied the west end of Main Street, squatting in and around the abandoned factories. Evelyn understood that many of the raggedy figures who floated like ghosts through the streets there were, in fact, just ordinary people with problems that could be solved. However, their presence in town often dissuaded new home buyers from settling in Baneford, painting it as unsafe. Long-time residents also avoided the industrial district, preferring to ignore blatant signs of their crumbling town than face the sad truth that something needed to be done.

Evelyn envisioned a redeveloped district brimming with retail, boosting the local economy. To help the homeless and win public favor, she suggested tax revenue from the project could be used to finance the establishment of transitional shelters elsewhere in town to care for and rehabilitate people from the streets. The mayor would be able to address the homeless issue and clean up a historic section of town in one go.

Evelyn also suggested that a portion of the newly developed space at Dyeworks be zoned for clinic use.

Baneford didn't have a hospital of its own, instead relying on Old Bedford Hospital for medical services. The lack of doctors and clinics in Baneford ensured the constant outpour of money to other towns. By offering clinics and medical service providers brand new spaces to lease, she argued Baneford could recapture some of that revenue while spawning a local industry.

The following morning, Evelyn held the report in her hands and felt proud about what she'd created in a short time. Less than a quarter inch thick, her report was not lengthy but included everything she believed the mayor would need to run his profit numbers. On her way over, she called Casey and made plans to see her for a late afternoon lunch.

At the mayor's office, Evelyn waited in the same reception hall. When Stewart came to greet her, she noticed that strange energy in him had intensified. The nervous spasms now extended beyond his mouth and awkward manner of walking. The convulsions shot up his back, shaking him, and he braced for each unanticipated tremor, trying not to tip over. The sweat on his brow and the pit stains under his arms were clear signs of his anxious agitation.

Foregoing any pleasantries, Stewart led Evelyn back to the mayor's office, where she noticed the door was slightly ajar. Stewart pushed it open and peered in, creating enough space for Evelyn to also see in the room and recognize the visitors inside. Seated across from the mayor, she saw Bill Oates, head of the town's zoning board, and Denise Sheeran, the town clerk. They sat with scotch glasses in hand, unusually early for that sort of thing, toasting and laughing loudly with the mayor. It was quite sinister-sounding laughing to Evelyn, giving her the impression that something wasn't quite right.

"I'm afraid the mayor's tied up right now," Stewart interjected, closing the door behind him. "I'll review these and get back to you. Let me escort you back out."

Stewart hastily guided Evelyn back through the reception area to the stairs, pushing her forward with his hand inappropriately placed on her upper back. She proceeded down the stairs and was relieved to feel his presence disappearing from behind her. Back on the street, she looked up at the building, perplexed. *Should I be concerned?* she asked herself, not fully sure what it was she suspected to be wrong.

At the office, Evelyn avoided interacting with her agents, still unnerved by the awkward visit. Trevor, Cam, and Sheryl were gathered at the back of the office, chatting casually, and she saw no need to dampen their spirits with her sudden anxiety. Instead, she planted herself at her desk and went through her unread emails. A few tedious hours passed before Evelyn heard a light tapping on the store window, where Casey signaled to her, dressed in her leather jacket and jeans, smiling.

"Thank God you're here," Evelyn exclaimed, rushing out to meet her.

Ducking into the Fairhaven Diner, they ordered diet sodas, neither being hungry and sat by the window overlooking the street, watching the people walking by outside.

"What's going on?" Casey asked.

"The mayor asked me to write a report for him."

"That means he's involving you in this project?"

"Yeah, it's just that… there's something creepy about him and his assistant lately. I don't know what it is, but I can feel it. It's like something's come over them."

"You're a beautiful woman. Men are bound to get weird around you, Evie."

"I don't think that's it. They're not hitting on me. It's something else…. Anyway, I thought we could walk over to Dyeworks, and I could tell you about some of what they're planning to do."

"Sure."

Walking down Main Street toward the industrial district, Evelyn and Casey passed many places from their youth, some teetering on the edge of bankruptcy, others already boarded up. Among those gone were Zone Arcade, where they played video games in high school, and Albion Skating Rink, where they'd both learned to glide on the ice as kids. On every block, they observed how worn down the buildings were, desperately in need of maintenance and repair.

Fifteen minutes later, walking at a brisk pace, they arrived at Dyeworks. Stopping on the sidewalk to take in the view, they looked up at the three-story building with its white clock tower and discussed how the site might appear after the work was done.

"You see the stone archways and that incredible brick façade?" Evelyn said, pointing out the detail. "They'll be able to preserve all of that with the exterior."

"Do you think they'll build on top of it?" Casey asked.

"They build behind it, adding a new tower directly in back of the factory. That way, they can keep the original shell. It'll be converted, along with the whole first floor, into a mix of shops and restaurants. Then there's going to be an office component and the residential at the top overlooking the town."

Casey looked at the sky over Dyeworks and tried to imagine the site. As they stood, the sun dipped behind the clock tower, casting a giant shadow over the street. Evelyn and Casey didn't notice the two homeless men wandering through the neighborhood until they were within earshot. Each wearing layers of sweaters and jackets, they walked slowly, weighted down by carrying what was likely everything they owned. One of them pushed a metal shopping cart filled with soda cans while the other staggered along, sucking smoke from the damp filter of a cigarette.

"Maybe we should go," Casey said, seeing them reach the other end of their block.

"They don't seem to be coming any closer."

The two men now stood on the sidewalk shoulder to shoulder, looking up at Dyeworks, same as Evelyn and Casey. They appeared transfixed by the building and remained motionless as they stared straight ahead at the factory in the shadow of the clock tower.

"That's weird," Casey said.

The one with the cigarette suddenly let out a long and despairing cry, like a coyote howling at night. Then, without provocation, he took off running directly at the building. Casey and Evelyn watched it happen. The homeless man collided with the exterior brick head-first, banging his skull against the hard wall at full force. They heard a cracking sound, and the man fell like a tree onto the pavement, straight onto his back.

"What the fuck was that?" Evelyn blurted out.

The other homeless man leaped into a frenzy, seeing his friend's terrifying outburst. He flailed his arms around, banging on his shopping cart and cursing loudly in the direction of the building. Catching sight of Evelyn and Casey, he paused momentarily before throwing his weight into his rattling cart and racing it away around the corner.

"Should we see if he's okay?" Casey asked.

Approaching the homeless man's body on the pavement, the first thing they saw was the blood trickling from his scalp, leaking from underneath his beanie. Though he'd landed on his back, his neck was turned violently to one side.

"He snapped his neck doing that!" Evelyn said.

Smudges of dirt coated the pale skin of his face. A short beard covered the jaw and chin, but his face was that of a young man no older than thirty-five. He died with eyes wide open and glassed over, staring right down Main Street in the direction of EM Realty.

Evelyn called the police and squad cars arrived with an ambulance following them. As the paramedics lifted the homeless man to a stretcher, the police officer on the scene came forward. He was tall, with a full head of light brown hair, and a square jaw. He introduced himself as Officer Ferry and asked Evelyn and Casey about what they'd witnessed and if they knew the deceased in any way. They gave the tall officer the truth, which was that they had no idea why or what had happened.

"Then there's nothing more you can do," said Ferry, exhaling deeply. "We'll look for the friend you mentioned, maybe he can tell us more."

"Will you please inform Lieutenant Crowley about this, too?" Evelyn asked. "I think he'd want to know that it happened here."

The officer clenched his teeth and looked away for a moment.

"He's in the back of the squad car. You can tell him yourself."

Evelyn marched over to see her friend and knocked on the rear passenger window, where she saw Ed seated, staring at the back of the seat in front of him. He rolled his window down and turned to face her.

"Hi Ed, I'm glad you're here."

"Yeah?" he asked. He did not smile or convey sentiment of any kind.

"I thought you'd want to know what happened, since it was at Dyeworks."

Ed looked past Evelyn at the ambulance, where the paramedics were closing the rear doors to their van.

"Doesn't matter," he said, rolling his window back up.

The tall officer got into the driver's seat, and the car peeled out, leaving Evelyn and Casey alone on the sidewalk just before dark. Evelyn feared that being close to death again would set Casey back on her progress. Unsurprisingly, she did not want to leave her apartment for the next few days.

CHAPTER 5

GRANT CALLED AT the end of the week, his voice coming through the speaker with a great deal of enthusiasm. He asked permission to show Evelyn a recent investment he'd made and for her company at dinner again. He communicated clearly and with purpose, which she found appealing, making her decision to say yes that much easier.

On the evening of their date, a cold fog settled in over the town. When she heard the limousine arrive outside, she went down and discovered that Grant was not in the car. Instead, he'd sent his chauffeur to bring her to the nearby town of Old Bedford. She sat alone in the backseat as the car navigated through the misty streets. Fifteen minutes later, the chauffeur pulled up to a newly constructed luxury home, a black and white contemporary farmhouse set on two private acres. Towering pines flanked the house from all sides, creating privacy from the outside world.

Evelyn exited the car into the garage and found that the house had a private elevator, which she took one floor up. When the doors opened, she saw Grant standing in the reception area, waiting for her with a glass of red wine in each hand. Dressed down from his usual suit and tie attire, he wore a simple Henley and jeans, giving him a much younger look.

"This is for you," he said, handing her one of the glasses. "Thank you for coming. I'm sorry I didn't pick you up, but I had to jump on a call last minute."

"That's okay; it was a short drive."

"You look beautiful as always," he said, with a glimmer in his eye. "I thought it would be nice to celebrate with *you* tonight."

"What are we celebrating?" Evelyn asked, looking around the room, unsure of the occasion.

"I just bought it," Grant said, inviting Evelyn further into the expansive living room. In the middle, two elegant and oversized couches sat opposite each other, around a central fireplace and entertainment wall. *He's talking about the house,* she realized. The windows went floor to ceiling, overlooking thoughtfully designed landscaping outside. The fog floated in and around the trees, providing a romantic but slightly eerie view.

"You bought this property?" Evelyn said, expressing shock at the size and elegant features of the home.

"That's right. I would have told you about it sooner, but it was a private deal. Off-market."

The interior had a sleek Scandinavian design, with clean flat surfaces and a minimalistic aesthetic. Yet Evelyn could see that every light switch, every fixture, every slab of stone, was of the highest quality. Abstract paintings adorned the walls, offering large splashes of color against the otherwise stark white canvas of the home.

"It looks like you're moved in. How did you do this so quickly?" Evelyn asked, looking around at the fully furnished space.

"The project in Baneford is going to be moving forward at an accelerated speed. I prefer to be closer for the time being, and I can't commute from my place in Manhattan. I had an offer out on this property before we met. My closing conditions were that the property be delivered immediately. My designer took care of the rest."

"Then I have to ask, why were you out looking at condos with Sam?"

"When I invest in a community, it's more than just the deal I'm looking at. I wanted to see how Baneford residents live. I want to understand the people, the culture, see how things function—at every level. Touring apartments with Sam gave me some insight, and I got to meet you."

Evelyn expected that Grant would see the world differently from her. Given his wealth and resources, he looked at things from above dispassionately, not swayed by desperation or need. Thus, Grant was efficient in his decision-making, and confident in his actions to bring about his desired outcomes. *They were able to convince the mayor to expedite approvals for the development*, Evelyn recalled.

Evelyn had never met someone as wealthy as Grant before. He was much less arrogant than she expected a person would be of his background, and she found it exciting to be with someone who possessed so much more knowledge and skill. As a driven entrepreneur, she wanted to learn more about his mind and how he approached both life and business. Evelyn inadvertently asked many questions, which Grant was happy to answer, leading her into the kitchen for dinner.

They sat at a marble kitchen island, and Grant served Evelyn "carpaccio on arugula with garlic crostini." She enjoyed hearing him say those words. It was followed closely by the main dish, spaghetti with black caviar sauce.

"Bon appétit."

"It's incredible," she replied, in awe of how delicious it was.

She picked up the noodles with her fork and rolled them in her spoon before savoring each bite, and Grant was pleased to see it.

After dinner, he invited her onto the covered patio overlooking the woods. The moon appeared as only a sliver of light, a waning crescent, in the dark sky.

"Are you excited that the project is moving forward?" Grant asked, leaning in closer.

"Yes, and I'm amazed you were able to acquire the land so quickly. I've never seen that much money exchange hands in such a short amount of time."

"Ursula wants to prep for site work this coming week, including demo and foundation. The latest rendering shows more net square footage than initially discussed. Coupled with Ursula's plan to preserve the front façade while adding fifteen additional stories behind it, the budget's easily going to top a hundred million."

It was a staggering number to consider, especially given that the person in charge of paying it stood right before her.

"You don't *just* want to be a realtor, do you?" Grant asked suddenly.

"I'm also a business owner, but of course, I'd want to be part of something like this and grow professionally," she said, feeling somewhat defensive. She'd always been considered a success story locally, but in comparison to what Grant was, she felt oddly embarrassed by his question.

"In my opinion, you're capable of doing big things. And you're an early supporter of our project. I'm sure professional and financial rewards are right around the corner for you."

"Thank you," she replied politely, not sure if his statement was meant to convey an opinion or a promise.

"It's the truth. That's why the mayor is also asking you to write reports for him. Maybe the Hyde team could benefit from your insights as well. I'll make sure they meet with you."

Evelyn hadn't gone on this date to win opportunities or accolades. Still, she was nonetheless extremely pleased and flattered that Grant wanted to involve her on the development side as well. It was not lost on her that Grant had the potential to be, among other things, the mentor she'd always needed.

At the appropriate time, Grant escorted Evelyn down to the garage, where he showed her his other new purchase, an Aston Martin One-77, probably the most beautiful sports car she'd ever seen, in a sleek silver finish.

"Get in," he said, smiling.

Driving Evelyn home, Grant zoomed through the commonwealth's old streets like he knew them well, undisturbed by the fog. He knew exactly when to slow down for sharp, in-coming turns and let the engine scream on the long, straight stretches. When he pulled over on Mox Street, Grant leaned over and kissed Evelyn. She felt the softness of his lips against hers.

"Thank you for a lovely evening," he said, pulling back, with the scent of his cologne lingering.

"My pleasure."

She shut the door to the car, and Grant sped off back home to the nicest house Evelyn had ever personally been in, as an agent or otherwise.

The following morning, Evelyn received a call from Hyde Properties. Speaking on behalf of Ursula, her assistant inquired if she'd be able to come to their Boston office that afternoon.

"Yes, I'll be there," she said, surprised that Grant had pushed the idea through so fast.

Evelyn arrived at an office tower in the Seaport District of Boston a few hours later. She checked in at reception and headed up to the twenty-seventh floor. The elevator doors opened, and she saw the name "Hyde Properties" printed in red and black on the sealed glass door. Before she could look for a button to ring, the door opened, and Ursula emerged, smiling, greeting her warmly.

Ursula led Evelyn to a conference room with floor-to-ceiling windows overlooking the harbor. Taking her seat, Ursula pressed a button on the table, and a few minutes later, the office assistant, a young man in a white dress shirt and black slacks, brought two cappuccinos and two bottles of spring water.

"You've managed to win the respect of Grant and the mayor in short time. Tell me about yourself. I'd like to know more about you," Ursula said, leaning in with genuineness in her tone.

Ursula wore her long black hair down today, and it fell over her shoulders in big wavy curls. With her casual attire and designer jewelry, she came across more like a rich housewife than executive officer, but when Evelyn looked into her fiery hazel eyes, she saw knowledge and experience looking back at her.

Evelyn told Ursula about her office, her agents, and the deals she typically worked on, trying to not sound apologetic. She knew it wouldn't impress Ursula in any major way, but Evelyn made it clear that she was a hardworking, hungry, and accomplished entrepreneur. With some delicate prying from Ursula, she continued talking, divulging more personal information. Evelyn disclosed that she did not have any living relatives, that she'd lost her father, Bruce, in an accident when she was nine years old, and her mother, Lia, to cancer almost ten years later.

"Even before they died, I was always driven... perfectionistic...," Evelyn said. "But it was never about being the best. It was about doing the best I could with what I had."

As she spoke, Evelyn felt the emotion coming across in her voice and realized she'd let her guard down too much. *Why am I telling her all this?* However, Ursula clapped, applauding her raw emotion and instilling her with confidence.

"That is what I sense in you, too. That energy can transform the world. Tell me about *your* vision for Baneford. I want to hear it right now," Ursula said, placing her fist beneath her chin.

Evelyn spoke about the things she'd put into the report for the mayor. She cited the transitional shelters for the homeless and the partitioning of office space for new clinics. Ursula's eyes grew wider the more Evelyn talked. When she finished speaking, Ursula shared back, speaking personally.

"I also lost my parents at a young age. I was on my own for many years, and I struggled to find my place. It wasn't until I staked my claim in the world that I stopped feeling alone."

Ursula painted a bleak picture of her early life. Her father left before she could form memories of him. Born to a middle-class single-parent home, she suffered as the only child of a drug-addicted mother with severe emotional instability.

"My mom would disappear at times, go on wild benders... Then she'd come home, sorry and apologetic, but then she'd do it again. Things were worse when the boyfriends came over. Some of them were animals... the things they did to a little girl... that's the life I had until she died when I was seventeen."

Evelyn learned that Ursula's early career offered her no respite from pain either. After a series of state-funded scholarships and grants, Ursula found a grueling corporate job where she worked for ten years before realizing it was a complete dead-end road.

"I had just gotten married and had my epiphany when we bought our first house. I was supposed to be fulfilling some common dream of owning property. It did not bring me the joy I expected. Even before we closed, I was thinking about the next thing. When I saw another house like the one I was buying, same size and layout, priced almost two hundred thousand dollars more, things clicked for me."

"You canceled your deal?"

"No. I flipped it for a profit and made more money in one project than I'd made all year at my corporate job. I quit that day. It wasn't long before I was raising money from investors, finding projects, and overseeing larger development ventures."

"That's how you started Hyde Properties?"

"The company came later, yes. Unfortunately, the marriage didn't last, but that first property is where I realized that I could do anything I wanted. I didn't need to do what others expected of me, and I certainly didn't need to take abuse from anyone anymore."

While Grant had influenced Evelyn to look at things from a distance, taking in the big picture, Ursula's message was about kindling the fire within. Ursula's story inspired Evelyn to break down the mental barriers of what she believed was possible.

"I want you to ask yourself what it is you really care about... what do you really want to do? In the meantime,

I'm going to present something formal to you to make sure you're an active player in this project," Ursula said warmly.

"I would love that," Evelyn replied, with gratitude in her voice.

When Ursula escorted Evelyn out, she hugged her at the door like an old friend would.

Evelyn returned home brimming with renewed hope and determination. For the first time, she contemplated a future far bigger than what she'd ever dared to imagine. In that projection, she saw herself as a woman with great wealth and influence, capable of acquiring whatever it was she really wanted.

Wishing to share her excitement, she called Casey and asked if she might like to join her that evening.

"Sorry, Evie. I have a date tonight."

"A date? Since when are you going out?"

"I know! It happened so fast. He's from out of town. I'll tell you about it tomorrow," she said, rushing off the line.

Evelyn was a bit disappointed not to have company that night but recognized how important this was for Casey. She was far too beautiful and too young to hide out at home alone, regardless of the horrors she'd seen. Looking for a distraction at home, Evelyn put on her comfortable clothes, sat in her living room, and continued her reading in Hurston Laurent's book, with slow blues playing softly in the background.

On top of being a real estate mogul, there was something unique about the way Laurent described his life. Like how

Ursula and Grant operated, he'd built his real estate holdings through developing connections with powerful people—something he said in a way that was neither boastful nor apologetic. It reminded her of Grant and his direct way of discussing money and business.

Almost an hour later, Evelyn heard a knock. She went to the door, certain to find Casey there, coming to spill the details after a first date. Instead, she found Grant standing in her doorway, dressed in his suit, on the way home from a late night at the office.

"Hi," she said, looking up at him, remembering when Adrian was at her door, standing a few inches taller than Grant did now.

"It's been a long day. I was passing by and thought it would be nice to see you," he said, leaning with one shoulder against the door frame, gazing at her with a childish glare in his blue eyes.

Grant's hair was slightly disheveled from its usual perfect state. He looked tired, but it made him more attractive because it made him human. Before the door could close behind him, he'd already taken her into his arms, kissing her passionately. She responded hungrily after the harsh absence of affection in her life. Her body shuddered as Grant's hands massaged the loneliness from her muscles.

"You're a stunning woman," he said between kisses.

Evelyn gave in to the moment and let Grant take control. By age and experience, he knew quite well how to please a woman and gave Evelyn his full attention as a competent lover. It didn't take long before they were in her bed, naked, with his body on top of hers. She could see the years of personal training in the separation of his muscles and the hardness of his body. He admired her curves, running his hands over all the places that excited him.

Evelyn wished to be loved again, but lying underneath him, she knew this wasn't what she wanted. She panicked, but he was already inside of her. *It's too late now*, she thought, surrendering to the act. The manner of Grant's affection changed as his excitement mounted, going from gentle caresses to pulling hair, slapping, and hard, forceful thrusting. Evelyn did not like it but could not find her voice.

When it was over, Grant dismounted to one side and wrapped his arm around Evelyn, pulling her close, communicating that this was no mere fling. She felt his breath slow down against her bare back, but her mind continued to race. She could not help but immediately worry about the professional implications of sleeping with Grant. *What will Ursula think?* she feared. *Can I say this was a mistake?* Grant did not seem to have the same worries, relaxed and comfortable there beside her.

"Mind if I stay the night?" he asked, further surprising Evelyn.

"Of course," she said softly, too conflicted to speak her mind.

Grant called his chauffeur and gave him clear instructions to go home and return early the following morning. With Grant sleeping beside her that night, his tan arm draped over her pale skin, Evelyn continued to ruminate, fearful that in one move, she may have ruined both love and her career. Realizing there was nothing she could do right then, Evelyn eventually forced her mind to slow down. Grant breathed quietly as he cradled her, and with the darkness of the room, she was lulled to shallow sleep.

Evelyn awoke early the next morning, before Grant, too early for there to be light outside. She crept out of the bedroom and escaped to the kitchen, where she sat on a stool facing the window, waiting for the caffeine from the coffee to permeate her bloodstream.

Grant joined her almost an hour after she'd gotten up, and she poured him a mug.

"I think maybe the next time I see you, we'll be in a business meeting," he said, smiling.

"Yeah," she said awkwardly. "We might be."

They sat awkwardly quiet for several minutes, with Grant sipping coffee and wearing only his boxers. When his chauffeur called, he answered and said he'd be out soon. Evelyn put the mugs away, and when she turned around, Grant was behind her. He pulled her very close and spoke in her ear.

"Maybe I need to have you again before I go," he said.

Grant kissed her neck, rubbed her breasts, and moved one hand down between her legs. When she felt it, she pulled his hand away and clamped her knees together.

"I'm sorry, I'm really not a morning person."

"Don't be like that!" he shouted loudly, standing up and towering over her. He pressed her against the wall and pushed his weight into her, holding her wrists. Evelyn closed her eyes. She heard a loud bang, like a door slamming shut behind him, and rapid footsteps. Grant's grip loosened.

When she opened her eyes, she saw Adrian. He stood in her kitchen, restraining Grant, with one arm pulled behind his back. Grant struggled to get free but could do very little, given the tight hold. Adrian looked at Evelyn with judgmental eyes, and she felt them burning her skin.

Adrian let go, and Grant stepped away and turned to get a better look.

"Who's this?" he asked of Evelyn.

"I'm sorry, Grant. This is an old friend. He thought you were… I think it's best that you leave."

Without saying a word, Grant went to the bedroom, got dressed, and left the apartment. Evelyn could hardly believe it. Adrian was in her apartment again, only hours after she'd slept with another man. She didn't know whether to feel embarrassment or rage. *This wouldn't have happened if you had stayed,* she thought.

"What are you doing here?" she asked Adrian, feeling defeated. *This was not how it was meant to be. This was not fair*, she told herself.

The judgment turned to a stare of indifference, and his brown eyes were distant. Other than the way he looked at her now, Evelyn saw the same tall, handsome, brooding man carrying the weight of the world on his shoulders that she'd come to love only last winter.

"Evil has returned to Baneford," he said. "I have seen it in my dreams. This time, you are at the center of it all. So, I have come to help us both."

He left the words lingering in the air and exited the apartment, leaving Evelyn alone, crying at the start of another day.

CHAPTER 6

WITH ADRIAN SO close, Evelyn's resolve was tested that week because she wanted to see him, but she did not seek him out. Summoned to a second joint meeting with Ursula and the mayor, Evelyn welcomed the distraction from her own thoughts, as well as the opportunity to contribute to the Dyeworks project. She got ready that morning, anxious to get out of the house but also fearful of how the night with Grant might affect things.

In the mayor's conference room, they were joined by Stewart and Annalisa at the wide boardroom table. Ursula spoke, and everyone nodded as if already in agreement with her.

"We want you to be our local representative," Ursula announced to Evelyn.

"Local representative?" she repeated.

"Schmooze the townies," Grant joked, to which Ursula shot a disapproving look.

"We'd like you to go to local businesses, schools, restaurants, your neighbors—the community—to educate them on what this project can do for the town. Invite them to go look at the building now and tell them about our plans. We want to be mindful of community feedback," Ursula said. "It's about garnering local support."

Evelyn was glad that Ursula was the one presenting this opportunity because the mayor's beady glances, Stewart's teeth grinding, and Grant's inappropriate stares were making her increasingly uncomfortable. However, Evelyn knew she could do this job well. She already knew many of the residents and local business owners, understood real estate and had always believed that Baneford deserved more. Evelyn saw how the Dyeworks project would be a blessing for the town and expressed her willingness to go door-to-door with the message if needed.

"I can do that," she affirmed.

"Excellent," Ursula said, clapping her hands once. "Please start immediately and report back when you've spoken to a sufficient number of people."

With that piece of business taken care of, Ursula and Grant shifted gears and discussed other matters with the mayor. They went on for a while, running through budget numbers, preliminary design approvals, and the town's requirement to include affordable housing in the residential unit mix. The mayor gave his consent for each item, with an attitude of the whole matter being beneath him.

"Does that work for you, Mayor Jenkins?" Grant asked.

"Sure, sure. That's fine. Let's move on," the mayor said, gripping the sides of the conference table tightly with both hands.

Grant's continued ogling from across the room made Evelyn fear others would notice. When Ursula began speaking about excavation, Stewart brazenly interrupted her, and the air went cold.

"Are you sure it's that spot? They've burst out in other places all over town. You need to move faster!" he blurted out, accusing Ursula.

"Be patient," she warned. "We're only a few feet down. I know it's there."

Evelyn listened to the words, but none of them made sense. *Who burst out of what?* she wondered.

When the meeting was over, Evelyn rushed out the door, overcome with a sudden feeling of relief at being alone. Before turning on the engine of her car, she slapped her thighs repeatedly, trying to dispel the worry from her body. *This is good news*, she told herself, trying to remain positive. Though everything still seemed fine, Evelyn felt like the danger was mounting all around her, but she could not see it.

Doing her best to keep these nameless worries out of her mind, Evelyn took multiple deep breaths and decided to focus on the job. The first step would be making a list of people and businesses to visit and discuss Dyeworks, with Casey at the head of that list, figuring she could practice on her friend before doing the real thing.

She called Casey on the way to the office. There were so many things she needed to tell her, and she could not wait to say them.

"Hey, can I come see you?" Evelyn started. "There's something that I—"

"I'm out of town for a few days," Casey interrupted.

"Oh, I didn't know. Are you with—"

"Yes, the gentleman I told you about. Terry," Casey said, sounding annoyed. "It feels so good to be away from grimy Baneford people."

"Alright, I hope you have fun. Any idea when you'll be back?"

"Hopefully never," Casey said, laughing, sounding like a bratty teenager, before hanging up.

Momentarily stunned by the strange call, Evelyn looked past the unusual attitude from her friend because it was most likely a joke she didn't understand or just some outburst stemming from all that Casey had endured.

At the office, Evelyn worked on her list, prioritizing businesses and established organizations first. She made calls for the rest of the afternoon, setting up meetings at the Baneford Public School, the police precinct, the library, local law offices, real estate offices, two non-profit satellite offices, supermarkets, and various other businesses she'd never spoken with before.

Passing by her desk, Trevor stopped to observe Evelyn furiously writing notes on her pad and scrolling through pages on her screen, fully engrossed in her work. He stood with his thumbs wrapped through the belt loops of his kakis, crotch hovering near her head, watching curiously.

"Is that for the developer?"

"They've asked me to go around town and garner support for the development," Evelyn replied, ignoring the bulge near her ear.

"You know what that means?" Trevor asked, smiling down at her.

"What?"

"New listings. I bet you'll get to sell some of those fancy new apartments they're going to build."

"Maybe."

"You will."

Evelyn heard the sincerity in his voice.

"I appreciate the support," she said, looking past the bulge.

If she did get the chance to sell dozens of newly developed condos, she'd need a team to do it, and Trevor was her most senior agent. Despite his occasional arrogance and blatant superficiality, she knew she could rely on him to handle business.

"When things progress further, we'll talk about the project more," she said. "Dyeworks won't just benefit me. It'll benefit the whole town and, of course, our office as well."

The next day, Evelyn went out for her first round of meetings. Spring showers hammered down on her car as she drove. With the heavy rain, visibility was reduced to almost zero, but Evelyn's windshield wipers swung at full speed, just fast enough to see the road. Fortuitously, when Evelyn arrived at her first destination, the rain stopped abruptly. She stepped through fat puddles as she walked from the wet parking lot to the main hall of Baneford's public high school.

Evelyn had attended grade school in the adjacent building, where she'd first met Casey, and together, they'd come here for the final four years of their pre-college education. Memories rushed back as she stood on the shiny hardwood floors again, worn down by many generations of stampeding children, smooth and glistening under the overhead light. Over seventy-five years of history were displayed proudly all-around Evelyn in the form of framed yearbooks, encased trophies, and hanging sports jerseys.

Headmaster Howard Bluff came eagerly down the hallway to meet Evelyn. He was a large, bear-like man, in his fifties, with a thick beard and head of hair. He wore a sweater over his dress shirt, stretched tightly over a voluminous belly hanging over his belt.

"Hello, Evelyn," he said with a deep and friendly voice.

"Thank you for meeting with me, Mr. Bluff," she said, shaking his hand.

Mr. Bluff escorted Evelyn to his office and asked her to sit down in the comfortable chair by his desk. He sat down in his office chair, his edges spilling out from either side.

"How can I help you today?"

"This is just an informational visit," she explained. "I was a student here once, and now I manage a real estate brokerage office on Main Street. I'm working with a developer who's planning to redevelop the old Dyeworks building. It has the potential to be a huge economic stimulus for the town. They've asked me to speak with town stakeholders to inform them about the project."

"That's very interesting," Mr. Bluff said, leaning back in his chair.

He listened to Evelyn talk about the project and the developer's vision, quietly stroking his chin and seeming pleased by what she had to say, nodding his head, and smiling intermittently. After she finished telling him what Ursula and her team intended to do at the Dyeworks, Mr. Bluff responded by sharing something that surprised Evelyn.

"I should mention that I'm from Saverill. I moved to Baneford for this job."

"Of course. That would be a far commute."

"Developers came to our town to do the same thing with our mill buildings a few years ago. They converted them into lofts."

"Yes, I remember seeing them on the market," Evelyn replied, demonstrating her knowledge of Massachusetts real estate sales activity. "They set a record north of the river for highest price per square foot at the time."

"They did more than that," Mr. Bluff said, leaning forward in his chair.

"What do you mean?"

"I was the principal at Saverill Public School at the time. When they started digging in the ground in and around the old mill buildings, some of our students got very sick. So did a bunch of people from the town. They never told us if it was environmental contamination or something else, but

I've always believed something went wrong there that we'll never know the truth about."

The thought of environmental contamination at the site was something Evelyn had briefly worried about before, given that the mayor had waived or delayed testing to allow for a quick sale to Ursula. She'd expected the headmaster to be pleased about the development, with the additional taxes meaning more school funding, never thinking this conversation would point back to that one detail.

"What happened to the kids?" she asked, horrified at the thought something similar could happen in Baneford.

"It wasn't anything the doctors could diagnose... The children became irritable, delusional, even violent in certain instances. Some adults around town were worse... especially those living closest to the development. Before we could do anything about it, everyone got better, and whatever 'it' was, went away."

"I'm so sorry that happened. I can't believe they never found out what caused it."

"Listen, I'm not saying that's going to happen here," Mr. Bluff added. "I guess as long as the development work is done according to state regulations, I shouldn't be concerned."

"So, you're not opposed to the project?"

"Well… no, not outright," he said.

"I'm glad to hear that, and I'm sure the town and developer will take all the necessary steps to make sure we're safe."

Considering him a potential supporter of the project and a good man, Evelyn thanked Mr. Bluff for his time. He insisted the pleasure was all his and spent the next several minutes telling her about the students, the new curriculum, and the ongoing renovation to the basketball court. Evelyn was pleased to see Mr. Bluff's genuine concern for his students. When the meeting was over, he escorted Evelyn back to the main hall and waved her off.

In the car, Evelyn took out her notepad and scribbled some notes, making sure to document what Mr. Bluff had said about the Saverill children before heading to her next appointment. The clouds threatened another downpour, but only a light drizzle accompanied Evelyn on the drive.

At the precinct, Officer Ferry greeted Evelyn and gave her the same grimacing expression she saw at Dyeworks before escorting her to the chief of police's office. She found Chief Rawlings sitting inside with Ed at a round table by the window. The chief was a stout but robust man with a thick black mustache and meaty cheeks.

"Come in," the chief said through a mouthful of food.

Ed did not bother to turn around. He and the chief sat at the table like stoned teenagers in their parents' basement, gorging on fast food cheeseburgers and onion rings while gulping down supersized sodas through thick straws.

As Officer Ferry closed the door to the office, Evelyn noticed a distinctly terrible smell in the room, which she suspected was body odor.

"Hi, Ed. Pleasure to meet you, Chief Rawlings."

"Have a seat," the chief said, waving her over to the empty seat at the table with his cheeseburger hand.

The closer Evelyn got to them, the worse the smell became. From where she sat, she could see the chief's dark hair was greasy, his ears overflowing with dark orange wax. He had sweat stains under his arms, dirt under his fingernails, and sleep crust at the corner of his eyes. Ed didn't look much better.

"How can we help you, Evelyn?" Ed said, taking another bite of his cheeseburger, the juices rolling down his chin.

"Well, Hyde Properties have asked me to inform town stakeholders about the development and report back with any feedback that might help them improve the project."

When he heard her say this, Chief Rawlings burst out laughing, spraying bits of French fry and saliva all over the table. Sweat accumulated on his brow, and his eyes bulged. It was as if she'd said the funniest thing he'd ever heard.

"It's great!" he choked. "We approve!"

"I thought that maybe I could speak with the people at your precinct so that I may get their opinions as well?"

"No need," Ed said, slurping his soda.

Evelyn didn't understand what was so funny, and she'd never seen Ed act this way.

"This development will affect the town in many ways," she braved. "It'll bring in money, but there's traffic and parking to consider, a homeless population in the area, and

I'm sure you have some concerns regarding safety and security," Evelyn said, desperately trying to engage them.

"They'll be fine," the chief muttered, still catching his breath.

"Thank you for the time," she said, standing up abruptly. They watched as she slowly backed out of the office.

What's wrong with them? she wondered, walking through the building and back out to her car. Putting the disturbing encounter aside, Evelyn was determined to finish her day strong and report back to Ursula with good news. She proceeded to her next appointment at the library on Main Street.

Two women stood behind the large librarian's desk at the front of the hall. They worked silently, moving books between piles and scanning barcodes on a computer. Evelyn asked for a minute of their time, and they stopped to listen to what she had to say. The older of the librarians was in her seventies, tall and thin, with thick, black-framed glasses and silver-gray hair pulled back in a tight bun. The shorter one appeared no older than thirty, with wooly blonde hair and oily, acne-prone skin.

Evelyn talked about the project itself, the potential tax revenue, and a couple of other ways the development could benefit the town. By the end of her talk, she sensed neither of the women was interested in the slightest.

"So, what do you think?" Evelyn asked.

She was met by silence, and only after an exceedingly awkward moment had passed did the older librarian attempt to respond.

"Well, good then," is all she said, signaling that the conversation was over. She returned to scanning books, and her young associate followed suit. *It's just not relevant to them*, Evelyn thought, excusing the rude behavior. She left the library feeling dejected, like an unwelcome salesperson, and walked back down the library steps to head to the next meeting.

At the offices of practicing civil attorneys Horowitz and Brown, Evelyn was fortunate enough to catch both partners at the office at the same time, and she saw very quickly that they were just as indifferent to news of the development as the librarians were. Brown looked away the entire time she spoke while Horowitz tapped his pencil compulsively on the table, squinting his eyes at her. Sensing their lack of interest, she argued that the project might pose legal challenges for the town, which might require their attention, but they were quick to shoot her down.

"Quite frankly, this development of yours has no bearing on our clients' cases," Horowitz said. "We don't care to be involved in any way at this stage."

Evelyn kicked an empty can down the street on her way to her next appointment, the first in a cluster of smaller businesses she knew well. Though discouraged, she mustered the enthusiasm to continue with her work. Evelyn hoped that people she knew, the managers of Grace's Bridal Shop, Hank's Ice Cream, and Lucky's Hardware, would prove more cooperative and express excitement for the project, or at the very least, a small level of interest just for the sake of being decent in conversation.

Grace's Bridal Shop opened on Main Street years before Evelyn was born. She recalled walking by the store with her parents as a young girl and peering in to see all the beautiful white gowns in the window display. Back then, residents from other towns would come to Grace's shop because it still featured some of the finest selections of handmade gowns one could find in New England. Today, however, Evelyn expected to find Grace's grandson, Herb, at the store with a ratty mullet on his head and a bottom lip bulging with tobacco. Unlike his family before him, Herb only sold knockoffs and secondhand dresses for the local crowd because the times had changed. The last time she was in the store, it had been with Casey, sometime during college, and it was Herb's ogling gazes that made them leave.

A bell rang when Evelyn pushed the door open and entered the store. No one stood attending to customers behind the glass counter, and there were no customers. Thinking perhaps someone might come, Evelyn waited and looked around at all the frilly fabrics and lace wear. Along the left wall, behind a glass counter, she saw Grace's best dresses. They hung proudly, looking over the other apparel like floating bride ghosts, propped up with safety pins and fishing line.

Evelyn heard a sound coming from behind the counter, rapid breathing accompanied by a faint clapping sound. Startled, Evelyn took a few steps forward to look behind the glass case. There, on the narrow strip of floor between the case and the wall, she saw Herb Trentino's bare white ass bouncing up and down. Underneath him, a middle-aged blonde lay on her back, with her dress pulled up around her shoulders and panties looped loosely around her ankles.

"Oh, my God! I'm sorry!" Evelyn said, looking away.

Herb and the blonde cocked their necks and peered up at Evelyn before responding in unison.

"Hi, Evelyn."

The blonde was Sheryl, and neither of them seemed embarrassed in the slightest. Herb continued to thrust between Sheryl's legs, which she kept spread wide on the dirty floor. With their necks turned around, staring at her, they appeared as strange moving statues in a wax museum. Evelyn took two steps back, and they remained as they were, fornicating on the floor with their eyes, wide and crazy, fixed on her.

"Excuse me," Evelyn said, quickly backing out of the store.

The bell jingled again as the glass door shut behind her, and Evelyn thought to herself again, *What the fuck was that?* She knew Herb had always been an odd character, but the sight of Sheryl, an agent from her own office, having sex on the floor like that made Evelyn wonder if she really knew anyone at all. So far, it had been a very strange day, and she still had two more appointments to go. For the first time, she questioned whether she had the resolve to see this assignment through.

With a troubled face and long stride, Evelyn walked next door to Hank's Ice Cream. A merry destination for Baneford residents, this sugary refuge was a staple of the town. Like Grace's shop, the management had reverted to the owner's next of kin, Bob Seward, son of Hank Seward. Evelyn remembered him as the jolly man who greeted children at the door with one hand on his rotund belly, the other waving them in, with his underarm jiggling in the air.

From the outside, Evelyn could see the entire length of the store. Red booths ran along one side, and a glass counter along the other. On and behind the counter, an assortment of cookies, pies, sugary treats, and ice cream cones was set up in impeccable fashion, like illustrations in a children's book. Soft-serve machines hung from the wall, and underneath them, refrigerated glass cases filled with buckets of ice cream.

She looked for Bob through the window, but he was nowhere to be seen. So, Evelyn went in to find him, to tell him about the Dyeworks project.

"Bob?" she called out. "Are you here?"

"Hold on!" she heard someone say from the bathroom.

A few seconds later, she heard a toilet flushing, and Bob appeared. Evelyn was shocked to see that Bob had changed considerably since the last time she'd seen him. His thinning red hair, which he'd always kept short, now fell around his shoulders in wispy strands, with the top of his head almost completely bald. By the looks of it, he'd gained *a lot* of weight. Bob was always heavy, but now he was twice as large and struggled to fit through the bathroom doorway.

"Evelyn. What's up?" he said in a tone quite different from the jovial one for which he was known.

"Hi, Bob. It's been a long time. How are you?" she asked warmly.

"Fine."

Not expecting any warmth or hospitality on this day, Evelyn dived into the purpose of her visit.

"A developer working with the town is planning on renovating the Dyeworks factory, bringing new apartments, retail shops, and commercial office tenants. I'm here today to gauge public interest, especially from nearby businesses that might benefit from the increased traffic in the area. We hope people like you want to be involved in supporting the project and sharing any ideas you might have about a massive renovation in the industrial district."

"That's fine," Bob said, walking over to the soft-serve machine.

Unsure if Bob was disinterested in the conversation or waiting for her to keep talking, she continued.

"Are you excited to hear that you'll probably have new customers coming into the store?"

"I'm hungry," Bob replied, grabbing his belly with both hands.

He reached for the back of the metal chair behind the register, pulled it over to the soft-serve machine, and sat down on it with his back toward the nozzle. Evelyn simply watched Bob now with a puzzled look, unsure how to interpret his behavior. The whole endeavor was filled with odd and unpleasant encounters.

"Am I boring you?" she snapped.

"No," he replied, apathetic in his tone.

He tilted his head back so that his mouth lined up directly under the soft-serve nozzle. With some finesse of his left arm, he reached overhead and pulled the silver lever to initiate the flow. A soft pink stream oozed from the nozzle and poured into Bob's mouth. He gulped intermittently without closing his mouth, allowing the sugary coldness to flow directly down his throat and into his stomach.

Bob kept the flow going until he'd consumed nearly a gallon of ice cream, at which point he pushed the silver lever back up.

"Gotta shit," he said, peeling his gelatinous body from the metal seat to head back into the bathroom.

When Bob closed the door behind him, Evelyn rushed to gasp for air, feeling the wind knocked from her lungs. *What the fuck is going on?* she kept wondering.

Evelyn only had one name remaining on her list, and she knew Mr. Moulton, the owner of Lucky's Hardware, very well. He'd known her parents, seen her grow up, and was now the sweet old man who was delighted each time she came into his store.

She saw him a few months ago when she and Adrian visited Lucky's looking for various odd items they needed for the ritual, which of course, they said nothing about. Mr. Moulton had been puzzled by the assortment of random inventory they purchased that day but was gracious, nonetheless.

Feeling confident that her last visit of the day would not be as creepy as all those that preceded, Evelyn went into Lucky's Hardware, eager to see a familiar, friendly face. She saw Mr. Moulton behind the counter, and he looked the same—white hair and mustache and the same kind eyes she'd always known.

"Evelyn!" he greeted her enthusiastically.

"Hi, Mr. Moulton. It's good to see you."

"It's always good to see you, my dear. What brings you in today?"

"I wanted to get your input on something. A developer has bought the old Dyeworks building and has proposed to redevelop it into a mix of apartments and commercial spaces. They've asked me to go around and seek input from key stakeholders in the town. You've owned this business for decades and have always been a cornerstone of the community."

"You're very kind."

"It's true. I also believe that the development will bring lots of people and attention to Baneford, which should benefit local businesses on Main Street."

"Absolutely, that makes sense," Mr. Moulton said.

"I can tell you all about the project, but in a general sense, would you say you'd support the revitalization of our industrial district?"

"Definitely. Baneford needs new buildings and new blood. Times are changing."

"I'm so glad to hear you say that," Evelyn said. "The developer plans to preserve the architectural integrity of the building and keep the façade. They will renovate the inside and build on the adjacent land. They plan to introduce class-A office space, which should attract new employers; there'll be ground floor retail and plenty of stylish apartments above on the higher floors."

Mr. Moulton nodded as she spoke, signaling he was paying attention, but Evelyn noticed that he'd begun tinkering with some items on the counter. As she spoke, he adjusted the muzzle of a nail gun, using a number of tools laid out on the glass. He kept a tin canister of rat poison nearby that released a noxious scent into the store.

"Other towns have had their development booms, and now it's our time," Evelyn continued. "This project will bring new tax revenue in, and we can use it to clean up our streets."

"That's great," Mr. Moulton said as he tussled with the screwdriver to break the nozzle free off the nail gun. "Sounds like it will indeed be good for everyone."

The piece of plastic he'd been loosening finally came off, bounced across the counter, and landed at Evelyn's feet. Mr. Moulton beamed a genuine smile at his gun. He reached for the box of nails and, using a pair of plyers, took the nails one by one and dipped them in the open canister of poison. He repeated this process over and over, setting the poison nails aside. Evelyn watched him, horrified.

"Why are you doing that?"

"Weapon."

"Why?"

"The fucking freaks," he responded without looking up.

Evelyn stepped back, concerned for Mr. Moulton, watching as he continued his work until he'd amassed a few dozen poisoned nails. He loaded them into a clip which he loaded into his gun. Finished, he brought the weapon to eye level and looked down the barrel.

"Mr. Moulton," Evelyn whispered. "Is now a bad time to talk?"

"Not at all. When do you think they'll start the work at old Dyeworks?"

"Well… I think they've started some of the groundwork, but the developer wants to hear residents' ideas before they finalize the construction plans, to make sure everyone's voice is heard."

"That's quite honorable of them, I have to say," Mr. Moulton said, looking down the barrel of the gun at Evelyn.

"I'm sorry, Mr. Moulton. I'm a bit nervous around guns. Would you mind pointing that away?"

"Damn it!" he shouted, slamming the nail gun down on the counter, shattering the glass. "It's not for you. I told you, it's for the fucking freaks!" he screamed.

Without a moment of pause, Evelyn turned, pulled the door open, and flung herself outside. She rested her back against the red brick façade, waiting for her heartbeat to slow down. A few pedestrians walked past her, unaware of her panicked state. She looked at each of their faces, looking for signs of danger because all around her, she felt people were changing, possessed by some strange energy.

Evelyn knew, better than most, that dark forces had the ability to manifest in all different ways. Only a few months earlier, she'd fought alongside Adrian to rid her town of an evil spirit that fed on pain and blood. She'd seen for herself the hauntings, the tormented minds, the devastation.

"What you suspect is real," she heard a familiar voice say.

Adrian stood beside her, leaning his back against the wall. This time, she noticed his hair was a little longer than it was before, and his strong chin now hid under a subtle beard.

"Why are you here?"

"You know why," Adrian said.

Evelyn wished to hear that he'd returned for her, though, in fact, she knew he'd come to summon the dead away. Across the planes of space and time, they beckoned him, and he answered the call. *He hasn't come for you*, she mourned to herself. Evelyn understood Adrian's curse, but she wished for him to ignore it, even for a short time. She wanted him to state his true feelings, then discuss things with her like an equal partner instead of leaving like a thief in the middle of the night. For the time being, however, it seemed there were more pressing matters at hand.

"What does it have to do with me this time?" Evelyn asked, thinking of the strange connection Adrian had discovered between her and Hendrick, the blood link.

"This time, I believe it is because of your work."

CHAPTER 7

TO EXPLAIN THE looming threat, Adrian invited Evelyn to sit down and talk. Evelyn went to her car and unlocked the doors. The mention of her work worried Evelyn because it was the one area in her life going well, and she did not want problems there. Deeper within, she feared what Adrian would say to confirm some of her darker suspicions. Certainly, she sensed something was amiss around town, and all the officials in charge of overseeing the Dyeworks development were, without question, acting strangely. More than that, something about Grant, and especially Ursula, seemed mysterious and out of reach to her. All the questions in her mind added to the anxiety and her regret for sleeping with Grant, Casey's recent attitude, Adrian's untimely return, and nearly being shot by Mr. Moulton; it caused her to scratch at her cuticles until they bled.

She sat in the driver's seat with Adrian beside her, like the last time they were together in her car before the fight against Hendrick, in which they'd both been nearly killed. Staring out the windshield, she waited for him to tell her what was going on. Outside, what little light shone through the overcast clouds dimmed and retreated with the hidden sun.

"You need to understand that real danger is coming, and its evil feels more powerful than anything I have ever felt before."

"What danger? What evil?" she demanded.

"I was far from here when I had the vision—figures in black performing a ritual. You were at the center of the circle. The ground opened, and there were voices in the depths… many of them."

"But I haven't seen any rituals… just people acting nuts."

"You are dealing with something far more terrible than you can imagine, and it is not just the dead. There are new people in your life recently?"

"I've been working with the mayor and a developer who's come to renovate one of our old mill buildings," Evelyn said, pointing down Main Street in the direction of Dyeworks. "Are you saying they're responsible for whatever is happening?"

Adrian looked into Evelyn's green eyes, expecting to see fear, but instead, he saw an intensity that he knew too well—a mix of curiosity and compassion—that told him she would not flee or hide.

"I do not know why people from your town are acting strangely, only that dark energies prey on the weakest of us—those of us who are not firmly rooted in ourselves. I also do not know who is responsible, only that their ill intention surrounds you."

"So, what do you expect me to do? I can't ask these people if they're evil, and I haven't seen anything to say they are!"

"What about the factory?"

"Dyeworks? What about it?"

"I believe the source of this evil is tied to a single place. A place where the ground opened, revealing a deep and endless chasm."

"I've been inside the factory. There's nothing like that there."

"Let me take a look. Can you take us there now?"

Breaking into Dyeworks was not what she had in mind, but with Adrian in the passenger seat, Evelyn went back west down Main Street and pulled in front of the old factory in short time. From their parked position, they spotted a lone homeless man with a gray beard pushing a metal cart nearby on the sidewalk. Two others, a man and woman, sauntered past across the street, frail under their oversized jackets. Further down on their side of the street, in the doorway of another abandoned factory, two men with clean clothes and bright sneakers stood watching for inbound customers and the police.

When the junkie couple approached the two men, all four of them exchanged words and nodded their heads before the woman dug into her jacket and handed over a fold of crumpled bills to one of the dealers. He, in turn, pressed a small plastic bag into her palm. When the transaction concluded, the couple continued down the street, picking up their pace, while the dealers went in the opposite direction, disappearing around the corner.

Having closed the distance, the man with the grocery cart walked past Evelyn's car, and they heard one of the wheels scraping against the pavement. It emitted an awful squealing sound, and because of the man's slow pace, the wheel sang for some time, screeching in their ears. Eventually, leaning into his cart, the old man managed to push hard enough to force the wheel to spin, rolling it away and fading into the distance.

"Let's go," Adrian said, seizing the opportunity.

Adrian led Evelyn toward the second front entrance, underneath the white clock tower, where Ed had let her in the first time. Unlike the main entryway's cast-iron façade, the door under the tower was made of wood and much less sturdy. Instead of picking the lock, Adrian leaned back and forcefully kicked it open, ejecting the padlock staples from the brick wall in the process.

"Let me go first," he said, entering the building.

Taking her hand, Adrian walked to the other side of the factory, where Evelyn had attended the first meeting. It was dark inside the building, and they tripped on bits of old leather and broken glass, walking toward the back of the building alongside the dye drums lined up at the center of the hall. Reaching the end, Adrian abruptly stretched his arm out to prevent Evelyn from falling into the giant hole at their feet.

It was about twelve feet in width and perhaps just as deep. It appeared someone had drilled through the foundation before digging down through the dirt underneath. Oddly, the tools and rubble had already been cleared away. With only a faint light coming in through the factory windows, Evelyn and Adrian could not see all the way down into the hole, though he sensed awful energy brimming underneath their feet.

"I've never seen development work start like this," she said. "Do you know what that hole is supposed to be?"

"I believe your friends want to access something underneath."

As they stared down into the depths, they heard a pattering coming from the direction of one of the dye drums.

"Did you hear that?" Evelyn asked, startled.

From the corner of her eye, she spotted a small figure in the shadows, hiding behind one of the drums, then she heard an odd clicking sound, like the squawking of a cicada. The figure scuttered away and disappeared down the line of industrial machinery.

"It cannot be..." Adrian said, with a bewildered expression on his face.

"What is it?"

Off to the side, something else made a rustling sound. They spotted it standing by the wall, partially concealed by shadows, with the shape of a short, stocky human with dwarfish arms and thick, muscular legs. It stood very still, watching them, but when Adrian stepped forward, the creature screeched and raced away into the darkness until their eyes could no longer follow.

The next one came right in front of them, visible in the pale light. No taller than a child, with wrinkled gray skin on its face, the beast snarled at them, revealing two rows of uneven razor-sharp teeth. Its eyes were like puncture marks, two horizontal slits in a hideous canvas of melted, dead-looking flesh. A strange crimson fur covered its body, prickly and slick, from the top of its head to its ankles.

This creature seemed to square off with them and rotated its shoulder blades back, exposing its leathery gray chest. It resembled a diminutive and hideous gorilla with the colors of blood and ash. Though Adrian seemed to know what they were, Evelyn quickly assessed that these were unfriendly creatures, minions of some malevolent force.

"It is a goheira."

"What is that?" Evelyn asked, her face tense with fear.

Before Adrian could answer, the goheira leaped high into the air, seizing Evelyn from above. It wrapped its stubby arms around her neck and sunk its teeth into the meat of her shoulder. Her high-pitched scream echoed through the dark hall as blood soaked through her sleeve.

Adrian grabbed the creature by its back, feeling its strange slick fur between his fingers, and hurled it away, like a soaking shag carpet thrown out to the street. It hit the wall, fell, and scampered away. At once, they heard the goheiras' clicking coming from all directions, and it grew louder.

"There are more of them. We must leave."

Evelyn nodded her head, holding one hand over her bloody shoulder. She turned to follow Adrian out. They proceeded back to the front of the factory, walking along the wall, trying to avoid being ambushed from behind the drums. In a flash of teeth and crimson fur, another one appeared, darting at them. It clasped onto Adrian's leg and gnawed on his thigh, tearing through cloth and flesh. Adrian cursed and slammed his fist down on the goheira's head, knocking it to the floor. He then kicked its little body away.

Not wishing to linger for a second more, Adrian took Evelyn's hand and rushed toward the door. Back on the street, Adrian and Evelyn jogged hand in hand from the clock tower to the car, with another cold rain beginning to come down.

"Let me drive," he said, seeing the amount of blood on her hands. "Do not worry. I believe I can heal our wounds."

Adrian steered the car hastily to Evelyn's apartment with the windshield wipers oscillating at full speed. When they arrived, he assisted Evelyn out of the car and took her inside the apartment to the living room. She sat on the couch in her damp clothes, with blood running from her shoulder and down her arm, horrified at what they'd seen. Adrian went to retrieve the first aid kit from its familiar place.

"Let me see," he said, returning with the kit in his hand. He assisted Evelyn in getting her shirt off over her head. "I heard stories in Romania when I was a boy about evil creatures that dig under the earth. Most of us believed they were just creations to frighten little children. In my travels, I have met others who swore to have seen them, but I never did until tonight. It is said they do not possess souls of their own; they eat human flesh, only come out at night, and are only found where dark magic and evil dwell."

Where the creature bit into Evelyn's shoulder, Adrian saw the imprint from the jaw—a series of puncture marks where the sharp teeth had penetrated.

"These cuts are deep, he added, dousing a cloth with peroxide to gently clear away the blood from Evelyn's shoulder.

"But what are they?" Evelyn asked, trying not to squeal from the pain.

"They are merely vessels," he replied. "Twisted incarnations of the evil energy that animates them. Something has caused them to manifest beneath the factory."

"But someone dug that hole."

"Because someone wanted to reach them, and what lies beyond. Possibly your new friends."

Evelyn looked down at her wounded shoulder, grimacing at the sight of it.

"If the stories about goheiras are true, earthly remedies heal the wounds they cause. Garlic bulbs grow underneath the ground," he said, darting into the kitchen.

Adrian returned with a garlic bulb in one hand and a plate and knife in the other. He peeled the bulb, then diced a handful of the cloves until they were mush. Scraping the garlic paste from the board and collecting it on the edge of the knife, he pressed the mush into Evelyn's wound, spreading it evenly.

"Elimina acest blestem," he whispered in Romanian. "Remove this curse."

The opening in Evelyn's shoulder frothed and bubbled for a few seconds, then a whisp of white smoke released itself into the air. When the bubbles cleared, the puncture wounds were gone, and her skin was completely healed.

"It is gone," he said reassuringly.

Dicing more garlic gloves, Adrian repeated the process, cut away the excess fabric on his jeans, and applied the paste to his injured thigh. The wound bubbled and healed just the same. Free from injury, they found themselves sitting alone in the apartment. Adrian could not help but awe at her beauty, and she caught the look on his face, the longing in his eyes.

Evelyn wished to tell him that he no longer had a right to look at her that way. *He refuses to say he loves me,* she said to herself. *Even if he can't stay, why won't he say it?* From Adrian's perspective, there was little choice in the matter. No matter what he said or did, a day would come when the dead would pry him away from her. For him, resisting the dead was futile. Their assault on his mind and the excruciating cacophony of tortured voices ringing in his head were too much to bear. Adrian had told Evelyn all of this before. That's why he would not make declarations, oaths, or promises because sooner or later, the dead would make a fool out of him. *Why say it if it will do no good?* That was as far as he could get.

"Come with me," he said, taking her hand and leading her down the hall.

He took her to the bathroom and, there, slowly undressed her. With each piece of clothing he pulled away, Evelyn's desire for him grew. But the feeling was tainted by the memory of Grant in her bed and her resentment at him for failing to acknowledge what she wanted most. Adrian turned the water on and waited for it to get hot before guiding Evelyn under the stream. He took off his clothes and stepped into the shower with her.

Adrian looked down at her, and she could see the affection in his eyes, the same as it was before. *But it meant nothing in the end,* she lamented, turning around to face the shower wall, refusing to look back at him. Evelyn realized that despite being naked with him again, as she'd been many times before, she could not pretend that she hadn't spent the last three months with a broken heart.

Adrian exited the shower stall, dressed himself in the fog, and she heard the door close as he left the apartment. Evelyn didn't know if he left because he was frustrated or out of shame, but she cried under the hot shower because this wasn't how it was supposed to go.

That night, with her head on the pillow, Evelyn's mind raced uncontrollably. Too much had happened too fast. She could not imagine the kind of implications what she saw at the factory had for the project, the town, and her relationship with Hyde Properties. In addition to the tension between her and Adrian, Evelyn felt that everything in her world was about to come crashing down.

At the office the next day, with the sunlight pouring in through the front window, Evelyn studied the behavior of two of her agents. Only Sheryl and Trevor were in the office, and each of them worried her deeply, albeit in different ways. Sheryl seemed to possess no shame over the previous day's unexpected rendezvous, while Trevor showed no concern for Cam's out-of-character absence from the office. He sat looking off to the side, admiring his own reflection in the darkened conference room window. Sheryl sat at her desk in front of him, scrolling on the computer with a smile so wide it was like she had clothespins pulling her cheeks back toward her ears.

"Oh, Evelyn," she said, grinning, "I think the market's slowing down."

None of the muscles in Sheryl's face aligned the way they should, given the circumstances. Yet she sat there with a look of smug triumph, paying no mind to the fact that only yesterday, she'd been caught ass naked on the dirty floor of Grace's Bridal Shop with Herb Trentino sweating over her.

"Rates are going up," Evelyn said in futility.

Evelyn briskly walked over to Trevor to avoid any further conversation with Sheryl. Trevor continued to study his own reflection in the window. He stood up, approached it, and combed his fingers through his blonde hair, smiling at the mirror image.

"Hey, Trevor. What're you doing?"

He turned around, not to respond to Evelyn, but to look over his shoulder and straighten the tuck of his shirt from the back. He ran his fingers over the creases in his dress shirt and slacks, making his reflection perfect.

"Our job is all about presentation. The way we look says it all."

"Where's Cam?" Evelyn asked.

"I let her go."

"Why?"

"Come on, Evelyn! She's frumpy, wears those hideous sweaters, those glasses, and... I don't want to mention the smell."

Trevor said all of this without breaking the stare with his reflection. Disgusted by the undiluted narcissism and self-obsession, Evelyn went back to her desk and buried her face in work. As she waded through emails and messages, she thought of Cam, sitting at home crying from what Trevor must have said, and Blake, wherever he might be. Evelyn had to consider the very real possibility that everyone she knew would be acting strangely soon, just like the others she'd seen. Further, she had no idea how to continue her job with Ursula knowing goheiras were burrowing under the factory at night.

A few hours later, Evelyn was pleased to see a call on her cell phone from Casey. She hurried out of the office to answer it, walking around the corner to a familiar stoop.

"Casey, are you back?"

"Yeah, I'm back. I'm with some of my new friends, and we're going to the park. I thought maybe you'd like to join us. Are you busy?"

"I'm at work, but I'd love not to be."

"Great. Then come meet us at Wollaston Park."

Eager to leave, Evelyn packed her bag and filled her travel mug with hot coffee. Sheryl and Trevor barely noticed as she went out the door.

Wollaston Park was one of the nicest public spaces in Baneford, not far from the Old Bedford border. Evelyn walked between the two stone columns that marked the beginning of the path Casey described. She proceeded past the freshly blooming cherry blossoms, along the winding path, down the hill, to where she came upon a clearing. There were several pairs of benches facing each other at the edge of the woods, under the shade of large maple trees.

Evelyn spotted three individuals sitting at the benches, Casey facing her and two others facing away. As she came closer, she was forced to hide her shock when she saw Grant and Ursula seated casually with her best friend.

"Evelyn, it's good to see you," Ursula said.

"It is good to see you," Grant said, standing up. "Please have a seat with us," he said, gesturing to the spot next to Casey.

Casey threw her arms around Evelyn's shoulders, hugging her tight. Unlike Trevor and Sheryl and everyone she'd interacted with the day before. The three of them seemed okay. Casey sat upright and alert, comfortable with her new friends. Grant and Ursula were calm and pleasant. It was hard to believe they were behind something as terrible as Adrian suggested. *But why are they with Casey?* That part seemed suspiciously not coincidence.

"I'm so glad you came," Casey said. "We were actually just talking about you."

"How do you all know each other?" Evelyn asked, trying not to look frightened.

"We met through Terry," Casey answered, smiling.

Evelyn remembered who he was the second she saw his face. Ursula's associate, Terry Pincher, whom she met at the very first meeting about the project, was Casey's new boyfriend. He came up and sat down on the other side of Casey, planting a kiss on her cheek. She took his hand and locked her fingers with his, like a young teenager in love. *That's not Casey*, she observed, recalling Terry's absence at the other meetings. *He's the one Casey left town with*, she realized.

"It's a small world. Isn't it Evelyn?" Ursula asked in a calm tone, seated across from her, enjoying the spring weather.

"Really small."

"That's why Terry and I took that trip!" Casey interrupted. "It felt so good to get away. I can't wait until you finish developing that building and bring some new life into this town."

"We're working as fast as we can," Grant laughed.

"We'd work faster if you hadn't kidnapped one of our associates," Ursula teased.

"She's a wonderful woman," Terry replied, squeezing Casey's hand tighter.

He looked exactly the way one would expect a person named Terry Pincher to look, but his pedigree shone brighter than his personality. Evelyn wondered how Casey had fallen for him because he wasn't her type at all. She watched them acting like small-town sweethearts and felt she could not recognize her friend.

Eventually, Terry broke away to discuss loan draw schedules with Ursula, but she deflected, preferring to focus on Evelyn.

"How are your public relations efforts going?" she probed.

Evelyn swallowed hard and tried to think of what to say. "I've talked to a handful of businesses. So far, there's positive sentiment, I think, but I still have plenty of people to reach out to, and I don't want to speak prematurely."

"But no real opposition or red flags?" Ursula asked, grinning mischievously.

"Nothing that I'm aware of," she replied, hoping to end the conversation.

Evelyn wished to know if Grant and Ursula really were involved in summoning evil from beneath Dyeworks. It was an insane idea, but she'd seen the goheiras and experienced their bite. If Grant and Ursula did have some culpability in the strange things happening in town, then she could no longer trust them. *That would also mean Casey is in great danger*, she realized.

However, operating on an entirely alternate wavelength, Casey proposed an idea to the group.

"We should all go out to Boston tomorrow night."

"That's a wonderful idea. You pick the place with Terry and Grant, but I'm in. Right now, we've got to get back to work. I'm sure Evelyn has plenty to do as well."

Ursula stood up first, and Grant followed, shooting a farewell glance to Evelyn on the way. Terry kissed Casey one last time before hurrying off with his colleagues. Evelyn and Casey turned toward one another.

"Where did you meet Terry?" Evelyn asked, trying to sound aloof.

"At my work. He came in for a personal training session, and we hit it off. He's strong! Did my toughest circuit like it was nothing. By the way, Grant and Ursula are so nice. You're lucky to be working with them."

"Casey, there's something you should know. Adrian's back in Baneford, and we went inside Dyeworks. There's something there. Something evil," Evelyn said, taking a pause. "There's a chance Ursula and her team have something to do with it."

"That's insane. There's no way any of them are involved in evil, Evie. There has to be another explanation."

"But you know this stuff is real. Hendrick was real."

Casey's expression grew stern when she heard the name, and her shoulders slumped forward.

"Where did you see Adrian?"

"I've seen him twice now. Things between us are so strange. He knows I slept with Grant."

"You slept with Grant?"

"Yeah."

"And?"

"It didn't feel right," Evelyn said, looking Casey directly in the eyes.

"Grant is handsome, charming, successful. I don't mean to be mean, Evie, but Adrian is… unique. How do you know he didn't just tell you a bunch of lies to get you back?"

"You know he wouldn't do that!" Evelyn snapped.

"I'm sorry. Just come out with us tomorrow night. With me. You'll see. There's a world outside of Baneford, away from evil spirits and all the townies. Let's have one good night. Please."

Evelyn thought about all her recent experiences in Baneford, with her agents, at the precinct, Hank's, Grace's, and Lucky's, and in a strange way, Casey was right. Getting out of Baneford, for even the shortest amount of time, would be good. Though Adrian was in town, she suspected there would be no shortage of horrifying nights to share together. In that moment of reflection, going to a fancy place in Boston with sophisticated people did sound better than an evening of being attacked by devilish beasts in the shadows of an abandoned factory.

"I'll come," she said, giving in.

CHAPTER 8

HOPING TO SILENCE the shouting thoughts in her head, Evelyn returned home that afternoon and sought escape in the pages of her book. Under the weight of her comforter, she continued reading Hurston Laurent's memoir, turning its pages until bedtime. She realized that Laurent's true message of the book went far beyond mere real estate. The wisdom he wished to impart concerned something else.

Evelyn detected a subtle moral stance underlying everything he said—good must triumph over evil. He illustrated this quite plainly several times when he described several pivotal life moments in which he was tempted to trade in his integrity for enormous fortune. Evelyn sensed by the tone of his words that he'd come very close to going down the darkest path. However, never succumbing to evil at all costs, Laurent argued, was the most important message he wished to impart. Though he did not say it explicitly, Evelyn read between the lines of his impassioned writing. Moved by his eloquence and intention, she read a passage aloud to herself.

"The privilege of outrageous wealth has not come at the expense of being true. I have seen darkness in people and in myself. I am thankful for never fully succumbing to its will. Those that have—and I witnessed them as they gave in to the darkness—the power they acquired came in direct proportion to the irreparable damage incurred on their souls. To travel along a path, straight and true, is what matters most. When I look at my grandchildren, I see what those who fell will never possess, and that is love."

When she was finished, Evelyn clicked the lamp off and rested her head on the pillow. *Am I on the right path?* she wondered. She knew Adrian was. Despite her anger with him, he was the only person she knew who did not fail at being real. Adrian stayed true to his word and lived in a manner consistent with his values, even in the strangest of circumstances. Walking the line that separates the living from the dead, he confronted horrors but did so with an open heart. Through all of his trials, and despite his shortcomings, Adrian did not stray from what he knew to be true, like a sailor following the brightest star across the seas. It's what she loved about him most.

The next day, Evelyn was relieved to find herself alone at the office. She spent the morning hours on the phone, prospecting and setting appointments. As she worked, she periodically glimpsed the open notepad on her desk containing the names of town stakeholders she'd intended to visit to discuss Dyeworks. There were still several people with whom she still hadn't met, and given how things had gone, she wondered if she ever would.

At noon, Cam walked in with her head down, chin tucked close to her chest. Knowing that Trevor may have said some horrible things to her, Evelyn immediately planned to remedy the situation. Trevor was not in his right mind, and Cam was as good an agent as any of them—she needed the support.

"I'll just pack up my things," Cam whimpered.

"Wait. I know what happened with Trevor, and I'm sorry. I think you're a wonderful agent and an asset to this office. I'm going to ask you to stay. You can help me with my listings until we get this thing sorted out with Trevor.

"Really?" she asked, fighting off tears. Cam knew how to list properties, manage photography, and deal with clients. She'd already dealt with all the lenders, attorneys, and inspectors. Evelyn realized that Cam was the perfect team member to help run the business during this challenging time—especially if Trevor didn't want her.

"Absolutely. I think it'll be a good thing for both of us to work with each other directly." Evelyn invited a less emotional Cam to sit beside her at the desk and went through her deal files. For upcoming and current listings, Evelyn granted Cam access to all relevant computer folders. One by one, she went over dates and details for each home, and Cam jotted her notes down. Evelyn found it surprisingly easy to delegate tasks to someone who already knew the business so well. Cam soaked up the familiar information, demonstrating mastery of the profession. They came away from their first session feeling really good about the collaboration.

"Thank you so much. I just couldn't tell everyone in Saverill that I was fired. I was so ashamed."

"You have nothing to be ashamed of," Evelyn assured her. "I didn't realize your family lived in Saverill."

"That's where my parents live. I still live at home," sounding slightly embarrassed.

"Do you remember a development in Saverill suspected of causing contamination?" she asked, wondering if Cam would remember the incident that Mr. Bluff had described.

"Yes. Why?"

"Tell me what happened."

"People got really sick. I was lucky I didn't get it."

"Sick, how?"

"They said something from the factory got into the water and made people act strangely. I don't think that's true, though."

"Why not?"

"Because the things that happened at the school... I don't think contamination could make children do what they…"

Evelyn stopped her when she noticed how uncomfortable Cam became. Instead, she focused on making sure Cam left the office that afternoon with her head held high. Shortly after she did leave, Evelyn heard the voices of several men shouting at each other outside.

Evelyn poked her head around the doorframe to see the action down the street. A small group of people stood where the explosion had broken through the pavement. Steel plates reinforced that section of the road now, and some of the individuals gathered there pointed at its surface.

"You hear that?" an old man at the front of the crowd asked from under his Sox cap.

"Sounds like electricity," a woman answered, holding her seven-year-old's hand tightly.

Evelyn listened intently for the sound they described. It took her a few moments to tune out the murmuring around her, but she heard it. At first, it was like the hum of a generator, but she realized it was chanting. Rhythmic and deep in tone. The pedestrians around her couldn't come to the same conclusion, but she was certain.

"Rats... an earthquake... people in the sewer..." they posited.

"I called the cops," Evelyn heard someone say from in front of the Fairhaven Diner.

A lone police car arrived, and it was Officer Ferry who exited from the driver's side. He hovered over the scene with an indignant attitude, bumping through the small crowd to get to the front. He hushed everyone so that he could listen to the sound under the steel plates. Satisfied with his determination, he announced that everyone was to depart from the spot immediately.

"What was it?" the old man asked.

"Absolutely nothing," Ferry shouted back. He stopped when he spotted Evelyn. "Good to see you again, miss," he said, taking off his cap.

"You can call me Evelyn."

"You work in this area?"

"Right there," she answered, pointing at the lettering on her window.

"I'll be sure to remember that," Ferry said.

"Have you seen—"

"Crowley?" Ferry interrupted. "He's in the back again."

Ferry turned in the direction of his squad car with a look of resignation. Evelyn went over and gently tapped on the rear window. When it came down, she could hardly believe what she saw. Ed had open blisters on his face and scalp, and they were angry and inflamed. One of them leaked pale-yellow pus down his forehead, almost to the arches of his eyebrows.

"Ed, are you okay?"

"It doesn't matter," he groaned from his throat.

Over the top of the car, Evelyn spotted Trevor running in the street, wearing only his boxers. Mr. Moulton trailed behind him, snarling, with the nail gun in his hands. Trevor jumped over the hood of a car and raced into the narrow alleyway by the diner. Mr. Moulton fired as he followed, muttering under his breath.

"Some things matter, Ed!" Evelyn yelled into the car as the window came back up.

Just before midnight, Adrian walked around the perimeter of the Dyeworks building, feeling a cold drizzle on his face. He looked for any signs or markers that might point to how the factory came to be occupied by such dark energy. He found none. In the distance, junkies and vagabonds drifted from one building to the other, but none came near, and no cars passed on the street.

For almost fifteen years, Adrian traveled the world communing with the dead, hearing their voices in his head. Here at Dyeworks, he could not only hear voices, he felt them too—a collective consciousness brimming with anger beneath his feet. Unsure how such an awful presence came to be located underneath this building, he suspected that at some time in the past, people practiced dark magic here.

Ever since the fight against Hendrick, Adrian's first confrontation with verifiable evil, he has felt his abilities evolving. Fighting alongside Evelyn, using the tools Maruf had given him, Adrian went from being a mere medium channeling the voices of the dead to the level of seer, capable of witnessing the past and isolated moments in the expanse of time.

Most haunting spirits were bound to this world by their sorrow, fastening their consciousness to the places where the worst moments of their lives occurred. Like his mother, Adrian possessed the ability to set the sorrowful dead free, unearthing their pain and severing their earthly binds. From there, the dead transcended to a place beyond sight, and the living were put at ease. That was always the life he'd been given.

But in meeting Evelyn, facing Hendrick, and investigating whatever lay waiting underneath the factory, Adrian was becoming something else. Instead of ferrying lost souls to peace, he now stood guard at the gates of the living world, offering protection from the evil dead. He'd never set out to be a soldier, but Adrian would fight until his last breath to protect Evelyn. It was innate, almost spiritual, the calling he felt to be her defense against harm. Though he could not say the words she wanted, in his heart, Adrian had already given his life to her.

Just as Adrian prepared to enter Dyeworks for a second time on his own, he noticed two ordinary-looking citizens walking away from the factory. They cut across the back lot and crossed the road, going toward a densely wooded area just north of the industrial district. They disappeared into the tree line, and Adrian followed them, curious to know what sort of activity transpired in the woods at this hour while keeping his distance to remain unseen.

Further in, the two men from the town joined a larger group of individuals lurking in the woods. They were just ordinary folk from Baneford, huddled like cattle in a field. Adrian found a spot from which he could spy on the scene undetected. He scanned the crowd, and though he did not recognize anyone, he suspected Evelyn surely would.

At home, preparing for a night out in Boston with Casey and the Hyde team, Evelyn asked herself repeatedly, *Why are you doing this?* While she still wanted to be part of something big, Evelyn was already beginning to doubt that Dyeworks would be the life-changing thing she'd always dreamed of. She feared Adrian's suspicions that Grant and Ursula were up to something terrible would prove true. Still, she hadn't seen sufficient evidence for it, which meant Grant and Ursula were innocent until proven guilty, and for the time being, she did not have to worry about Casey being alone in the company of psychopaths.

Outside, a black limousine sat waiting. Climbing in, she found Grant and Ursula sipping champagne on the black leather sofas, with Casey and Terry touching inappropriately opposite them. Ursula slid over, making sure to move the hem of her black dress out of the way, creating room in the middle for Evelyn. Grant pulled the sides of his sports blazer together and slid in the opposite direction, making space on the other side. Casey's lips continued to travel across Terry's face as he stroked her thigh up and down. Evelyn squirmed in her seat, seeing her friend act this way, but she was glad to see Grant handing her a glass of champagne. *To relax my nerves,* she assured herself.

"To good company! Cheers!" he said, raising his glass.

Everyone raised their glasses, and empty flutes were refilled. Leaving Baneford, they merged onto the I-93 highway going south to Boston. Evelyn sipped her second drink more slowly than the first, losing herself in the motion of the car, with soulful melodies playing in the background and the city skyline growing larger out the window.

"What's this place we're going to called?" Casey asked.

"I believe it's called 'Alibi,'" Terry said.

"That's right. A friend of mine owns it," Grant said, smiling. "Converted it from an abandoned office building to a club five years ago."

The limo stopped in an unsuspecting alley in the financial district, flanked by midrise office buildings. Bouncers dressed in black ushered them from the car to the back entrance of a discreet-looking building with no visible signage on its brick exterior. In the back stairway, Evelyn could hear music thumping loudly in the building, shaking the walls with deep bass. Together, they passed through the swinging double doors at the top of the stairs, entering the spacious VIP balcony overlooking the exclusive club below.

Alibi's main level consisted of a massive dance floor at the center and a stage for DJs and performers running along the front wall. Bar stations and seating areas circled the dance floor, and bottle-service girls prospected through the crowds. On the balcony level, guests in the VIP lounge enjoyed direct access to the vibrant energy of the club from an elevated and more comfortable distance.

An attractive female attendant with high cheekbones and a short skirt greeted Grant and escorted him and his party to the special table he'd reserved. It was the one closest to the railing, offering an unobstructed view of the action below.

"Please make yourselves comfortable. I must introduce Ursula to some of my investors," Grant said, gesturing to a bunch of suits drinking whiskey at the other end of the balcony.

Grant took Ursula's hand, and they glided over to the investor table, where he introduced her. She charmed her way through the group, helping to secure vital capital pledges well before the official demo date. Evelyn watched from a distance, noticing how each of the men softened in their postures as soon as Ursula spoke to them, their body language revealing all. *It's her natural talent*, Evelyn surmised, *to make people follow.*

While Evelyn took these mental notes, Casey and Terry sat next to her, whispering sweet nothings in each other's ears, excluding her from any possible interaction. In the absence of coherent conversation with her best friend, Evelyn sought solace in the strong drinks. Sometime between the third and fourth drink, Fred and Analisa joined the table.

"We took the long way," Annalisa said, seeing Evelyn's confusion, to which Fred nodded in agreement.

When Grant and Ursula returned, excitement was written across their faces. More money for their development. Relieved not to sit alone anymore, Evelyn stepped out of character and sparked a conversation.

"I didn't know people did deals in places like this."

"Deals are about people," Grant smirked. "Business can take place anywhere people with ideas and money are gathered."

"That's why we like you, Grant. You see the big picture," Ursula said. "We've closed deals in places you wouldn't imagine under the wildest of circumstances. But we always win because I have a secret."

"Yes, yes, your big secret," Grant teased. "When do I find out the secret to your real estate success?"

"I'm glad you asked. I've spoken with my colleagues, and we think very soon," Ursula said mischievously.

Evelyn rolled her eyes when she realized they would not be hearing Ursula's secret that night, though she found it curious Ursula knew things that Grant did not.

"Well, I hope I've proved my competence thus far," Grant said, trying to sound modest.

"Speaking of competence… I want to see all of you on the dance floor," Ursula said, changing the conversation and taking Evelyn's hand.

She led her across the balcony floor to the stairs leading down. The others followed, holding onto each other's arms to avoid getting lost in the crowd. They came together on the dance floor, creating a small circle in a sea of people, and had their fun. Ursula swayed to the music, whipping her long black hair around. Grant stepped to the beat beside her, feeling the rhythm in his feet. For being older, both Ursula and Grant were much more fun than Evelyn had expected. Seeing them dance, she wondered if maybe she was being too uptight around them for no reason. Meanwhile, Casey writhed in Terry's arms. Analisa danced gracefully on her own, and Fred, the oldest and frumpiest of the bunch, snapped his fingers and wiggled his shoulders, at which Evelyn grinned.

The harder she danced, the more her worries slipped away in the whirlwind of sound, people, and color. Grant moved away from Ursula to dance with Evelyn and took her hands in his. Tipsier than normal from mixing drinks and less inhibited after starting to dance, Evelyn was flattered by the attention and danced back at Grant in an increasingly seductive manner, brushing her body against his. It made her feel powerful and free, so she wanted more.

Evelyn didn't see it happening, how she and Grant were beginning to act quite like Casey and Terry. She took his arms and wrapped them around her waist, spinning in place, using her hips to tickle his lap. Evelyn ran her fingers through Grant's thick, silver hair and pulled his face close. She kissed his lips and pressed her tongue to his, ignoring the world around them. She was surprised to see Ursula smiling at her because, normally, this was something that would have embarrassed her deeply.

The dance floor led to more drinks, and passions continued to rise. Emerging from a haze of lights, music, and pheromones, Evelyn found herself back in the car again. She saw Ursula and Grant's grinning faces on either side of her. Casey and Terry sat across, entangled, as was becoming usual. Traveling back north along I-93, with music blaring and drinks in hand, Evelyn's buzz led to a distinct and intense arousal in her body. With the vehicle swaying gently along the highway, that desire compounded.

Unexpectedly, the car made a stop on the way. Ursula rolled down her window, and Evelyn saw Fred and Analisa there, standing in front of a wooded area with their limo pulled up to the curb, hazard lights flashing.

"There's a delay," Analisa whispered into the car.

"There can't be!" Ursula shouted. She exited the car immediately. "Go!" she commanded of the driver before shutting the door.

The chauffeur seemed to know what was happening because he rolled up the window and took off again, leaving her, Fred, and Analisa alone on the side of the road with the other car. Before she could make sense of things, Evelyn found herself back at Grant's house, sitting beside him on one of the sprawling coaches in the expansive living room.

Casey and Terry continued to fondle each other on another couch. Evelyn found it slightly amusing when Terry began to remove her friend's clothes until she was completely naked. The next thing she knew, she and Grant were watching them have intercourse. Then Evelyn felt Grant's hand under her dress, between her legs, and it felt good. Her mind searched for a reason why it shouldn't but failed to think of a single one.

Grant kissed her neck, and she closed her eyes, so the room would stop spinning. She didn't remember spreading her legs wide for Grant or agreeing to have sex in front of her best friend. When he entered her, Evelyn opened her eyes and looked over at the other couch. Terry's naked body heaved over Casey's. They scratched and howled at each other like animals in heat. The smell of sex permeated the room. Evelyn went in and out of awareness. Once the pleasure faded, it was followed by a heavy fog that led to a vacuous and dreamless sleep.

Adrian hid behind the thicket of trees and watched the townspeople gathering in the woods. Coming together in the middle of the night, one or two stragglers at a time, they grew in number, about fifty in total, huddled closely together, staring off into the distance. They did not show signs of coordinated activity and, for the most part, just rested there like sheep for over two hours. Intermittently, a pair of them broke away to have sex on the forest ground. Others engaged in short bursts of fist fighting, always inevitably forgetting what it was that offended them and returning to the huddle as if nothing had happened.

Not having prepared for a long night outside, Adrian zipped his jacket, tucked his hands in his pockets, and observed the bizarre spectacle without making a sound. Almost three hours after he'd first come, three hooded figures arrived, their faces concealed under the black cloths, and he sensed the show was just about to begin.

The hooded figures proceeded to the center of the congregation and walked straight through, with the townspeople parting, allowing them to take their place at the head. Adrian noted the hierarchy among them and the welcoming of their leaders. Before the hooded ones could address their followers, an energy seemed to travel the crowd, causing a stir and inspiring some of the townspeople to chant. Adrian heard the low-octave hum and knew something terrible was about to happen.

One of the townspeople, a young man with blond hair, came forward carrying a flaming torch in his hand and gave it to the hood on the left. Then, a blonde woman stepped forward, approaching them. She looked to be about forty, with an antiquated hairstyle and plastic smile. Adrian did not recognize her, but this was Sheryl from Evelyn's office, and they commanded her to her knees.

The hood in the middle stepped around Sheryl and pulled her hair back, exposing her neck, then removed a dagger from within the black robes and cut Sheryl's throat. As the blood spilled forth down her chest, spraying from her neck, another energy moved through the crowd again, but this time, it started at their feet. The goheiras appeared, waist-high in the crowd, scurrying forward with piranha jaws.

They surrounded Sheryl on the ground, emitting their syncopated and unnatural clicking sounds. Their frequencies grew louder and echoed through the woods. The goheiras viciously ripped pieces of her flesh away, eating her body as it lay. Adrian could not believe the site, but it was the townspeople that scared him the most, with the light from the torch flickering on their faces. *None of them are looking away.* If ordinary people could watch their neighbors be eaten with complete apathy, things were much worse than they seemed.

CHAPTER 9

EVELYN AWOKE ALONE on the couch in Grant's apartment and barely recognized where she was. She strained her eyes to look around the room, not yet adjusted to the early morning light coming through the windows. Evelyn saw Casey spread out on the couch at the other end of the room. Grant and Terry were nowhere in sight. A revulsion arose inside her, moving from her stomach to her throat, and the memory of the night before came flooding in. She quietly tiptoed across the living room, hoping not to vomit.

"Casey, wake up," Evelyn whispered, trying to jostle her friend awake. "Wake up!"

"Go away," Casey mumbled, hiding her face in the corner of the couch.

"We have to go."

"I'm staying."

Desperately wanting to get Casey out of there, Evelyn realized she wouldn't succeed without causing a commotion, and she certainly didn't want to see Grant or Terry, or anyone else. She looked down at her friend passed out, facedown on the couch, and forced herself to slowly step away. It felt cowardly to do so, but she picked up her purse from the floor and made her way to the front door.

Outside under the bright sun, Evelyn walked across the landscaped property, trying to get off the grounds as quickly as possible. She passed the tall evergreens separating the front yard from the street and continued traveling on foot for several minutes until she'd put ample distance between herself and Grant's house. From there, she called a taxi to bring her home.

As she rode in the backseat of the car, images from the night before flashed in her mind. Evelyn could not fathom how she'd let herself be with Grant again and in that way. It was times like this she needed her best friend close, but Casey was gone. *Something in the drinks?* she asked herself. The taxi pulled up to her building, and Evelyn handed the driver cash. Eager to get to her apartment and hide her face in shame, she did not expect to see Adrian. He stood in the hallway by her door, surprised to see her entering in such a frazzled state.

Shame boiled through Evelyn's veins, and she could not bring herself to look him in the eyes. She let Adrian in without saying a word and left him standing in the kitchen by himself, going directly to her bedroom and shutting the door behind her. On the other side, she cried, choking on her sobs, trying to stifle them so he would not hear her.

Evelyn peeled the clothes from her body and wished she could do the same with her skin. Under the hot shower, she scrubbed hard, trying to wipe yesterday's memory from existence. She stayed until her fingers pruned and the bathroom was white with steam.

She returned to the kitchen a short while later and found Adrian sitting on a stool, staring out the window. Beside him, fresh daffodils sat in a jar on the counter, popping their yellow heads over the brim. *Fuck. Did he bring me flowers?*

"What're you doing here?" Evelyn asked, approaching timidly.

"Last night, I saw the ones responsible for the strange curse on the town," he said, looking away. "Many are affected. I came to tell you."

"What happened?"

"Three people dressed in black hoods killed a woman and fed her to the goheiras... in full view of fifty people from your town."

"Did you see who they were?"

"No. But I believe it is the people you have been working with. Were you with them last night?"

"Yes."

"When the hooded ones killed the woman, it was about three in the morning. Were you with them then?"

"I don't know... I'm not sure... maybe," Evelyn muttered, unable to recall what time anything happened the night before.

Adrian nodded but said nothing, looking at her with pity and sadness in his eyes. Evelyn felt the pain of his incriminating stare. In her heart, she felt awful for what she'd done last night because of him most of all. Breaking his heart with another man was the last thing she wished to do.

"You're not going to ask me where I was?" she asked with a shaky voice.

"Why should I?" he shouted, swatting the vase suddenly, shattering it against the wall. Adrian had the capacity to have his heart broken and continue fighting, but he could not hide his emotions forever.

Startled, Evelyn flinched and stepped back, her heartbeat thudding loudly in her ears. Adrian looked down at the flowers and glass shards on the floor and refused to look away until she'd left the room. Evelyn feared he'd never look at her again as she turned to walk out. She wanted him to scream at her, to berate her, call her names, anything except shut her out.

Taking a minute to cool off, Adrian retrieved the dustpan from the broom closet and cleaned up the mess. Sweeping the kitchen floor, he felt, more than ever, deep resentment for how his life had turned out. He hated the rules by which he was forced to play the game. Adrian pitied himself as a cursed man, doomed to wander, barred from ever having a home. He wished desperately for a way to stay with Evelyn, but there was none that he knew of. If he dared to remain in one place, the voices of the dead would come, shouting in his head, driving him mad. The endless cycle.

For the time being, however, the voices had stopped. Adrian knew his time in Baneford would not be indefinite, so he'd need to move fast to make sure Evelyn was safe, and yet, they still had no idea how any of the strange things they'd witnessed came together. Adrian set aside his emotions for the work at hand. He joined Evelyn in her home office, composed and rearranged. He spoke only of Dyeworks, and Evelyn understood he had no intention of asking her whereabouts the previous night. She listened as intently as she could, fighting through the pain. However strange it was, Evelyn was happy to hear that Adrian had a role for her in his plan. *If nothing else, we'll have that time together*, she told herself.

Adrian did not want to take Evelyn into danger, but he needed to go inside Dyeworks and summon the past. It would involve several minutes of being quiet with his eyes closed, unable to defend against goheiras or anyone else that might be lurking. Having seen construction equipment on the site the night before, taking Evelyn there just before dark made the most sense, early enough to avoid the goheiras but late enough to avoid the crews. She would have to stand guard while Adrian used his ability to search for the origin of the strange power overtaking the town.

"What do you need me to do?" she asked, quivering at the thought of seeing goheiras again.

"If the stories are true, goheiras can be killed just like any other beast. We will bring weapons, and you will have to stand guard."

Adrian gave Evelyn a rough idea of what he intended to do. They left the apartment in the late afternoon, with plenty of light remaining in the sky. Reluctantly, Evelyn drove the car back to Lucky's, remembering how twisted and insane Mr. Moulton had been. Hearing the story of what happened, Adrian promised to go in alone.

Adrian went in to see Mr. Moulton standing behind the shattered counter. He'd placed a wooden board over the top but left the shards of glass all over the floor. As Adrian came closer, he noticed the old man had dark circles under his eyes, bruised knuckles, and his clothes were dusty and torn. Whatever it was he'd been doing, it had not been peaceful.

"Are you one of the f-f-f-fucking freak-k-k-ssss…," Mr. Moulton stuttered, saliva spraying from his mouth.

"No, I am not."

Mr. Moulton looked Adrian up and down, squinting suspiciously.

"If you are, I'll f-f-f-fucking k-k-kill you."

"I understand," Adrian replied, curious to examine what manner of possession this was.

He felt an alien energy in the old man's body, surging with immense power but absent of personality. Mr. Moulton was not possessed but entranced, and whatever malicious energies flowed through him congregated in the most primal parts of his consciousness. The spell consigned him to an almost animalistic state, and Mr. Moulton, typically of an amicable nature, responded with violence and paranoia.

Reflecting on how the townspeople behaved in the woods, all of them had devolved in the same way. They were also entranced, Adrian realized, each person engaging in the vices that were most natural to them. This was the reason townspeople were acting strangely, fornicating with each other at odd times, in inappropriate places, fighting, and self-harming, but also responding apathetically to the world around them. It explained why no one had turned away at the sign of Sheryl being eaten by goheiras, a sight that, under normal circumstances, would have made the average person sick.

Since there was no spirit in Mr. Moulton to set free, Adrian focused all his energy on reaching his soul and reviving it from its dormancy. With his hand on Mr. Moulton's shoulder, Adrian reached deep into the old man's memories, looking for something to remind him of his true self.

With his eyes closed, Adrian could still see the outline of Mr. Moulton, the shape of his body tucked away behind a thick, black veil. Adrian tried to pull it away, his hands grasping at the material in the vision, but his fingers passed through it as if it were made of air. Up close, the veil did not appear to be made of any fabric but instead, a dense layer of black smoke, shifting and hovering over the old man's body. Unable to pull this shroud away, Adrian attempted the opposite by walking directly into it, disappearing into the dark haze. At the other end, he saw a tall woman with long black hair standing over Mr. Moulton. Whisps of black smoke circled around them like scavenger crows. Adrian sensed a desperate hunger about them. Though the woman cast the spell, it was these spirits circling the room that bestowed the power, and they were the ones making the townspeople act like animals, ready for slaughter.

Mr. Moulton's body began to shake. Adrian opened his eyes and held his shoulder firm, determined to bring the old man out of his trance. He needed to remind him of something important, like someone he loved, to overpower this spell.

"What is the name of your eldest child?" Adrian shouted at the old man, guessing he'd been a family man.

"Layla."

As soon as he said the name, his face softened. Adrian could feel a bit of Mr. Moulton's soul shining through. He focused on that piece and fed it strength. In the same way that he connected with the dead to set them free, he used his ability, for the first time, to bring a living person back to themselves. A familiar glimmer returned to his eyes, and Adrian pulled his hand away.

"I'm here to pick up some supplies."

"Tell me what you need, and I'll see what I can do," Mr. Moulton said in a pleasant tone as if their initial exchange never happened.

Adrian listed the items he needed, and Mr. Moulton went about the store, fetching everything and bringing them back to the plywood countertop. Adrian paid the old man and wished him a good day, unsure just how long this moment of clarity would last.

"Okay, take us to the factory," he said, jumping in the passenger side after putting his supplies in the trunk.

Evelyn went down Main Street, and they arrived at Dyeworks roughly two hours before sunset, early enough to avoid the goheiras and hopefully late enough to avoid any construction people on site. Planning to park the car on a nearby side street, they went around the corner and saw that the construction crew was still there on the back lot with hard hats on and the excavator ripping through the rear of the building, tearing down a sizable section of the exterior wall.

To avoid being seen, Evelyn continued driving past the building, and Adrian guided her to the edge of the woods, where he'd gone spying on the townspeople the night before. She parked the car on the empty street, out of sight of the factory, and got out of the car. From this distance, they could still hear the hum of demolition equipment. Adrian popped the trunk and grabbed his supplies. He led Evelyn into the woods to his familiar hiding spot. It was a small patch of grass surrounded by a thicket of trees on all sides, providing the perfect place to move about and remain unseen. He dropped the two duffle bags and began to remove the supplies, laying them out on the ground.

Evelyn watched curiously as he spread the bizarre matchup of items out for her to see—two axes with long handles, a twenty-five-pound bag of sodium chloride salt, multiple rolls of black duct tape, batteries, and four high-powered ultraviolet flashlights. He removed the UV lamps from their packaging and wiped the axe handles clean of dust so the duct tape would stick better. Then he taped one lamp to the bottom of each axe handle, pointing down, and one right under the axe head, pointing out. This way, no matter which way they held the weapon, the light would shine in two directions at all times.

"If we wait too long for the construction men to leave, the goheiras will be there when we go inside. It is best that you are comfortable using it." Adrian got up off his knees and handed Evelyn one of the axes. "Hold it like this," he said, with one hand low on the handle, the other higher near the head. The light will shock them, but you must swing the axe to kill them."

Evelyn turned on her UV lights and held the axe forward. She practiced swinging it in different directions, getting a feel for the weight, coming back to center after each strike, and glancing back at him for approval.

"That looks very good," he said, holding back so much. From where Adrian stood, he saw the woman he loved with an axe in her hands, proving to him yet again that no other woman in the world could compare.

Being in the woods with Adrian reminded Evelyn of the first time she'd been alone with him, at one of her listings at night. *When I found out ghosts are real*, she joked to herself. After saving her life, he made her feel loved in a way no one had before. His love was the powerful magic that had protected her during the most terrifying moments of her life. Now, on the precipice of another battle, Evelyn feared she'd never get to feel that connection again.

When the sun had almost disappeared over the tree line and the sky was nearly dark, they headed back to Dyeworks on foot and heard no sound coming from the factory. Adrian and Evelyn held the axes close to their bodies, out of sight, with the lights turned off. Drawing closer to the building, they saw the construction crew had gone home.

Adrian led Evelyn through the lot and over to the part of the wall the excavator had knocked down, slightly wider than a double door. They looked in both directions before entering, ensuring no one was there to follow them. Inside, they came upon the hole.

"The goheiras will not come until after the sun has set. We should move quickly." Adrian said, holding the bag of salt with one hand, an axe in the other.

Gripping her weapon tightly, Evelyn saw that the hole was now much bigger, several feet wider and deeper. *They must have brought the excavator inside.* Looking around, between and around the dye drums, she confirmed no goheiras were present. The factory was perfectly still.

Close to where they stood, a metal staircase led to the mezzanine level floating high above the factory floor, looking down from all sides. It was comprised entirely of offices with tall glass windows running along the inner perimeter of the building. Adrian gestured for Evelyn to go up first and followed behind her, sprinkling a trail of salt on the ground.

"Why are you doing that?"

"Salt purifies and preserves. It is essential to life and will repel them."

Ascending to the top of the stairs, they walked down the open corridor, looking through shattered windows and broken doors. Adrian stopped to go into one of the offices, with windows and doors still intact.

"In here," he whispered, sprinkling salt across the floor. "What I need to do requires me to sit down and close my eyes. I will not be present with you, so I will need you to stand guard."

Adrian showed her where he wanted her to stand, close enough to the window to see the floor below but far enough away not to be seen. Moving toward the back wall, Adrian pulled a rusted metal chair out from behind the old desk and placed it in the corner. He sat down and closed his eyes. Without an object or person to use as his compass, he focused all his energy on the building's past. By the time Evelyn turned around, he'd already slipped away, his eyelids fluttering and axe resting on the ground.

A symbol flashed in Adrian's mind. He saw the tribal depiction of an animal—a dog or coyote, drawn abstractly with wavy, frantic lines. He perceived something sinister about it as if it were a bad omen.

Evelyn heard footsteps below. Seconds later, she saw someone walking into the factory alone, wearing a black robe with the hood drawn down, covering their face. They stopped beside one of the old dye drums and peered from a distance into the hole. Evelyn watched suspiciously from above, hoping no one else would come. Adrian's body shuddered when the next vision came to him.

Out of the shadows, he saw an indigenous man approaching. He had dark skin and long black hair. He wore a crown made of feathers, but his spirit was heavy and sorrowful. The man held a knife in his hand, with a handle made of bone and a coyote symbol etched into the side and colored in red. When three sisters approached, modestly dressed and ill-equipped for the wilderness as the early European settlers were, the chief offered them the knife. They were of light hair, innocent in age and experience.

Two more hooded figures walked onto the factory floor and took their place beside the first. Evelyn looked back at Adrian, but he still had his eyes closed.

The youngest of them took the knife from his hand. At once, Adrian saw the indigenous man disappear, and an old colonial house came into focus. It was set near a wooded area beside a gentle river. The three sisters went into the house and closed the door behind them. Though he could not see inside, Adrian sensed something awful encroaching upon them, a looming curse already set in motion.

He opened his eyes to Evelyn, who was looking at him with concern.

"They're here," she whispered.

He crept over to her, and they stayed low, peering through the open door and under the railing to observe the events below. Several townspeople slowly filtered into the dark space. When about a dozen had amassed, one of the hooded figures spoke over them.

"We are your servants, and we have come to honor you," said a woman, sounding quite like Ursula.

The crowd chanted back at her, a low octave hum, the same word over and over.

"Shun-kah, Shun-kah, Shun-kah, Shun-kah."

Evelyn's stomach turned when she spotted Casey in the crowd. And beside her was Stewart Dinklage. In his fidgety, anxious manner, he reached his scrawny arms into the crowd and pulled a man forth. Evelyn recognized who it was—Mr. Bluff.

"Oh my God, it's—"

"Shhh."

The hooded one in the middle stepped forward, unsheathed a dagger, and ran it across Mr. Bluff's throat, cutting it open. Even from the mezzanine, they could see the blood spraying out, painting his face and hair red. More blood leaked down his chest and onto the floor at the edge of the hole. That's when the goheiras began to appear, crawling out from the darkness of the pit.

When they started eating at Mr. Bluff's body, Evelyn turned away, biting her fist not to scream. She breathed through the terror and forced herself to look down again. The robed figures removed their hoods, and Evelyn finally saw the truth for herself—Ursula, Fred, and Analisa's familiar faces emerged from under the black cloth. Evelyn also saw Terry brazenly standing in the crowd by Casey's side, but not Grant.

Ursula raised the knife and licked the blood from its side, then turned to leave. The goheiras slowly began retreating into the hole, carrying what remained of Mr. Bluff with them. The crowd followed her out of the building through the hole in the outer wall, and in a matter of minutes, Evelyn watched the last of them trickle out of sight.

"We should go now," Adrian said, seeing the goheiras were gone, too.

Adrian and Evelyn ventured out from their hiding spot and walked along the mezzanine aisle toward the metal stairs. When they reached the staircase, even stepping quietly, it rattled under their weight, with fixtures no longer fastened securely after decades of neglect. The clanking sounds echoed through the empty hall, and before they could reach the bottom, two goheiras had crawled out of the hole and stood together in the moonlight. The creatures made their clicking sounds in synchronicity, staring straight up at Adrian and Evelyn through their slit eyes. Their crimson fur glistened in the light, but their gray, leathery faces were as pale and lifeless as death.

"I hate these fucking things," Evelyn blurted out, only a few steps from the bottom.

Adrian and Evelyn raised their axes and clicked on their UV flashlights in anticipation of the landing. As they stepped off, one of the goheiras came forward. It squealed as the salt burned its tiny feet. The goheiras curled their upper lips back and exposed their razor-sharp teeth. Using its short but muscular legs, one jumped high to attack Adrian at face level.

"Get ready!" Adrian shouted, pointing his flashlight at the creature.

It shrieked in pain and fell to the floor before it could reach him, covering its eyes, and Adrian split the beast in two with his axe. At once, its body withered away into ash, leaving no trace. The other goheira jumped up and sailed higher than the first, clear over Evelyn's head, and landed behind her. With the second torch on the axe pointing in the opposite direction from the first, the creature was caught in the light head-on and shrieked. Evelyn held her breath as she twisted her torso to swing the axe, decapitating the goheira. The severed head and lifeless body both turned to ash.

Three more goheiras appeared near the back corner, blocking the way to the outside, clicking obnoxiously at them. Two bolted forward, scurrying directly at Adrian over unsalted ground, while the third goheira jumped to the scaffolding, trying to attack from above. Adrian and Evelyn used their lights to keep them away and slowly backed out of the broken exterior wall.

Relieved to be outside, they quickly walked to the car, holding the axes low, looking over their shoulders, hoping the goheiras would not follow them out. Putting the weapons away in the trunk, they heard a sound coming from the woods. Fearful the goheiras had come from a different direction, Adrian stood guard, ready to defend. Instead, she saw Ursula emerge from the tree line, wearing her black robe with the hood pulled down.

They stopped when she saw them and just stared over the short distance, but her gaze hit them like a laser beam.

"Let's go," Evelyn said, clenching her teeth.

Ursula emitted a hysterical laugh, shrill and loud, before retreating into the woods.

By the time Adrian reached the passenger door, she was gone.

CHAPTER 10

EVELYN CLENCHED THE wheel tightly as she drove back to her apartment, worrying about all the things she now knew. Ursula was responsible for bringing all the evil to Baneford, and she had seen them outside the factory tonight. Evelyn glanced over to the passenger side and saw a look of dismay on Adrian's face as well.

"Did it work? Did you learn something that can help us?" Evelyn asked, looking for any reason to feel hopeful.

"I saw things, but I cannot piece them together… an indigenous man… the symbol of a coyote… and three young women, sisters, receiving a strange gift."

Adrian wished he had the ability to cut forward to the end and tell her everything, but it had never been that way. With multiple threats closing in and plenty still left to uncover, he recognized how difficult the way forward was.

"I wish my friend was here to help us," Adrian said as they pulled up to Evelyn's building, thinking of Maruf and his unique knowledge of ancient curses. "He would know what to do."

She heard the self-doubt in his voice. Adrian carried the duffle bags into Evelyn's ground-floor apartment, where he placed them on the kitchen counter. Seemingly, out of nowhere, he started breathing rapidly and frantically, as if in a state of shock. Evelyn dropped her keys and rushed over to him. His body trembled, and his breaths were choppy and hysterical.

"Adrian, are you okay?"

He could not respond, only gasping in response. Adrian could not explain that he felt a sense of impending doom. His heart thudded, and his mind fixated on one terrible idea—*you have already failed her, and soon she will be dead.* He lived with the guilt of having left once, breaking Evelyn's heart, and he could not bear the idea of failing her again. Saving her was the only thing he'd done right, and the thought of losing her meant more than just losing the woman he loved; he'd lose the last shred of his own remaining humanity, too.

After a few minutes, with Evelyn's hand on his shoulder for comfort, Adrian was able to slow his breathing and center himself.

"I am sorry. I do not know why that happened," he said, embarrassed by his episode.

Adrian wished he could tell her how he truly felt, but from his perspective, it would only cause false hope and pain. Still, he sensed something different about himself, and he was unsure what it was. It did not feel like a connection from the other side. Instead, it was an amplification of his primal emotions, starting with fear and slowly blossoming into a steady, burning anger.

There were many things Adrian had license to be resentful for. Most of all, not being free to go where he pleased because of the dead constantly summoning him. If he refused them, their voices grew louder in his head, filling it with pain and noise. He could not escape his own head, and it was an awful way to live at times. The one thing that offered any reprieve was the longer he stayed actively using his gift, communing with the dead, the longer the periods of silence would last. They were neither long nor consistent enough to be measurable, but to a man serving a life sentence, a week here or there without being summoned felt like a holiday cruise.

"You didn't say where you were before you came to Baneford," Evelyn said, thinking that maybe something had happened to him during the months he'd been away.

"I was in Egypt, lifting curses and performing exorcisms with my friend Maruf. One night, I dreamt of you and heard many voices calling out in the dark. As you know, I answer when the dead call, but I was very grateful to know that I would see you again."

"Were you happy in Egypt?" Evelyn asked, wishing to understand him better.

Sadly, by this stage of his life, Adrian had already lost hope that he'd ever be truly happy. He wished to be with Evelyn, but he could not. *Of course, I wasn't happy,* Adrian fumed. *If she must ask me that question, she does not know me at all.*

"I wasn't happy!" Adrian shouted, overcome with anger, slamming his fist into the wall and damaging the cement board. Evelyn jumped back.

She was suddenly terrified. She'd never seen Adrian so angry, and for the first time, she was intimidated by his size and stature. He appeared intensely agitated, shifting his weight from side to side, cracking his knuckles compulsively as if gearing up for an alley brawl. Risking him not hearing her at all, Evelyn said one more thing, and it wasn't a question. She hoped it would make him say what she desperately needed to hear.

"I'm grateful knowing I get to see you, too."

Adrian heard it and stopped. These kind words were enough to temper the brewing storm of fear and anger deep within. He could see the sincerity in Evelyn's eyes, and it nearly brought him to tears. He wished to say the words she wanted to hear most, but he could not bring himself to say them because of the false promise they bore. Adrian could not profess his love.

Evelyn left Adrian brooding in the kitchen and went to the living room. Preparing a spot for him to sleep, she tucked fresh sheets into the couch, threw a comforter over it, placed a pillow at the head, and dimmed the lights. She retired to her bedroom alone. Of all the ways she'd imagined their reunion, none were as tragic as this. She felt deep sadness seeing Adrian in pain, with no way to reach him, despite how strongly she felt for him. Resting in different rooms, sleep did not come easy to either Evelyn or Adrian because of how unnatural it felt to be apart yet so close at the same time.

Not too long after they'd lain down, Adrian heard noises coming from outside on the street, the shuffling footsteps of a large man, followed by the sound of a car door slamming shut. Adrian peered through the living room blinds and saw a man just a few feet away at the building entrance. Adrian quietly went to the bedroom and woke Evelyn up.

Returning to the living room, they peered through the blinds together. Evelyn saw that the man was Bob Seward, an odd person to be lurking outside her door. When the second car pulled up, they noticed it was a police vehicle, and it was Ed Crowley who got out of the driver's side to join Bob at the door. Ed wore his uniform sloppily, shirt untucked over sweatpants, no cap to conceal the raw blisters on his thinly covered scalp. They wrestled with the lock until they managed to open the door.

As they entered the building, Evelyn and Adrian heard footsteps and labored breathing in the hallway. *We shouldn't have come back here*, Evelyn realized. With little time to think, Adrian feared what he might have to do when Ed and Bob entered the apartment. He didn't want to hurt them, but if they tried to hurt *her*, he would do whatever necessary. Adrian primed his nervous system for violence, and he waited for them to come crashing through the front door.

"Come this way," Evelyn whispered, pulling him away from the living room to the kitchen, snatching a set of keys from the counter.

Behind the kitchen's main door that rested open on its hinges was a secondary exit to the apartment. He'd never noticed it before. It opened onto the back stairwell leading out to the street and one floor up to the late Mrs. White's apartment above. Evelyn took Adrian up to the unit, using her keys to quietly sneak inside. It had a mirror floor plan to Evelyn's apartment, so Adrian knew where to go. He went to the living room window, hoping to see Ed and Bob's eventual departure. They stepped carefully on the hardwood floor, mindful to not draw attention upstairs. Evelyn waited in the foyer of the apartment, by the front door, listening for any footsteps coming up. A few minutes of silence passed where neither Evelyn nor Adrian knew what they were doing downstairs, but it wasn't too long before Adrian spotted their two hefty silhouettes exiting the building and leaving in their separate cars.

Sneaking back into her apartment in the middle of the night, Evelyn was alarmed to see several missed calls on her cell phone from both Grant and Ursula during the time she'd been upstairs. *I have no intention of calling either of you back*, she thought to herself. Adrian looked out the window one last time to make sure the street was empty before going back to the couch. Evelyn came and sat beside him, and he draped his long arm over her shoulder, pulling her in close. Occupying a space meant for one person, they were more comfortable here than they were before. She nestled her body close to his, he held her tight, and for the first time since he'd been back, they enjoyed the warmth and comfort of each other's company the way it was meant to be.

Waking up next to each other the next morning, Evelyn and Adrian were grateful. He opened his eyes to the most beautiful sight he knew and wished every day could be the same. He loved having her so close and could not hide his joy as he thought about how quiet and sweet it was. Evelyn saw the familiar look on his face, and in this moment, it was enough for her to relish in the admiration.

Unfortunately, in stark contrast to the waves of love floating through the apartment that morning and the bright sun outside, they recognized the town was filled with turmoil and potential enemies. They were now unquestionably in unfriendly territory, evidenced by the break-in last night, so soon after seeing Ursula in the woods. With so many people entranced by Ursula and the dead of Dyeworks, Evelyn and Adrian discussed the importance of moving through town undetected, especially considering they needed to visit the public library next, a busy and central spot.

Adrian only had fragments from a vision to go off. Still, he intended to search through old books and historical records for clues that might tell him why the dead of Dyeworks were tethered to the factory and how they'd come to be so evil, summoning goheiras and calling for blood sacrifice. He wished to understand Ursula's true motives for casting a spell on the town. The idea of finding any relevant information at all at the library would have seemed insane to Evelyn had she not been down this road with him before. It was entirely possible that some written record spoke of Dyeworks' history or alluded to the darkness inside.

Evelyn and Adrian were careful not to be seen leaving the apartment. They parked behind the library, away from the main road, and scanned the scene before going around the corner, up the stairs, and into the expansive hall filled with books. From one end to the other, rows of bookshelves ran along the entire span of the floor. In between them, long and narrow isles formed; roads in a land of ink and paper.

To the right, the librarians Evelyn spoke with before sat behind the main desk, entering books into the system with their handheld scanners. Evelyn and Adrian proceeded down one of the middle aisles and arrived at a reading nook.

Seeing no familiar faces around, they set their things down at one of the wood tables and began their search. Starting in different sections of the library, flipping through all sorts of books, they amassed a collection at their table—local history, occult stories, world symbology, spiritual practices—anything that might offer a helpful clue. Even with the risks, Evelyn was oddly joyful to be at the library with Adrian that late morning. In a room filled with millions of written memories cataloged and stored to bear the breadth of time, she felt that *this moment* mattered, too.

Amassing two healthy piles on the table, they ceased searching and started skimming. Adrian looked through his books with angst, racing against time, slapping the pages as he turned them. Evelyn flipped through hers at a steady pace, approaching the task with an air of patience. It took over an hour for them to exhaust their piles, finding nothing worthy of further investigation.

They returned to the shelves to start the process over again, and the longer they searched, the less likely it seemed they would find what they were looking for. But they persisted and carried more stacks of books to the table when the previous pile had been combed through. The task grew increasingly tedious as the rounds went on until Evelyn came upon something striking. In a book she'd already forgotten the title of, she spotted a symbol that looked like what Adrian had described. She held the book open with her finger on the page.

"Did it look like that?" Evelyn asked in reference to Adrian's vision.

He jumped in his seat when he saw the picture. The tribal rendering of a coyote composed of thick wavy lines.

"Yes! Which book is this?"

Evelyn turned the cover around to show Adrian the title, *Native American Tribes of New England*. It featured the image of a traditional Wampanoag hut, with a running stream in the background, and discussed the history, culture, and spirituality of the Wampanoag people. Then, flipping back to where she'd stopped, Evelyn quietly read some of the text out loud.

"In 1615, the incoming Europeans brought something far more devastating to the New England natives than what any army could accomplish. It was smallpox. Entire villages were lost because of native tribes' nonexistent immunity to foreign pathogens. Before the century was over, the Wampanoag had grown wary of visitors."

She and Adrian looked closely at the coyote symbol in the picture. It was painted clearly on the side of a white ceramic bowl. Under the photo was a caption.

"The coyote is a supernatural being in Native American spirituality," she continued reading aloud. "Believed to be a deceiver, or trickster god, with the power for both creation and destruction."

"We need to find something else," Adrian said dismissingly, slapping the table with his palm. "There must be a connection to the factory itself. By what means did such dark power come to be located there?"

Evelyn heard the anxiety and agitation in his tone. This wasn't the Adrian she had known, impulsive with his moods and ill-tempered; she remembered a man who'd stayed calm even during the most difficult situations. Still, she heard his concern. *Something had to lead back to Dyeworks.*

Since it was a commercial building, Evelyn had forgotten to do the one practical thing she was trained to do and did all the time—look up property ownership history. She left Adrian at the table, fidgeting in his irritability, and logged into a nearby computer. Searching through Massachusetts land records, she found an old document referencing the Dyeworks address and the town exercising its right of eminent domain to acquire private property for public use. She returned to Adrian with the printed record in her hand.

"In 1802, the city of Baneford, in the Commonwealth of Massachusetts, hereby appropriates 11 Main Street by eminent domain. Past owner of record: James Wildes," Evelyn read out loud.

"What does that mean?" Adrian asked, looking up from his new pile of books with bloodshot eyes.

"11 Main Street is the Dyeworks address. This paper says the city took ownership of the property over two hundred years ago. But the Wildes family were the original owners. It was a single-family home, once. That's the first record in the file."

With a name to search for, they went back to the local history section, searching for title records with mention of the Wildes family, starting with when the property was first recorded in 1684. In one book, cataloging key documents from the old town archive, Adrian found the copied photograph of a public announcement made in 1702. Signed by the representatives of the colonial government, the message mentioned the mysterious disappearance of two of the three Wildes sisters, Susannah, and Rebecca, daughters of James Wildes, a local landowner and widower. Adrian read the last line of the announcement to Evelyn.

"We hereby regretfully confirm that James Wildes has committed the gravest of sins in taking his own life."

"If his daughters went missing and he killed himself, who got the house? The third sister?" Evelyn asked, confused by the strange dead end.

At the end of their research, they still didn't know how all the pieces came together. There was Ursula and her team, the goheiras, the spell over the town, and a very specific reason why all of it revolved around Dyeworks, but the most important piece of information was still out of reach. Adrian wished to continue searching in the library, but Evelyn felt there was something else she needed to do.

"I know Casey is under their control," she said. "Do you think we can help her?"

"We can try," Adrian said, shutting the book in his hand.

Though he'd only been able to lift Mr. Moulton out from under Ursula's spell temporarily, Adrian believed having Evelyn near might produce more lasting effects for Casey. Their life-long relationship would act as the tether to her true self, rooted in love, more powerful than Ursula's efforts to reduce the townspeople to an animalistic state.

A straight shot south from the library, they arrived at Casey's building, and Evelyn eagerly rushed to the entrance, hoping to find her friend. Adrian followed closely behind and saw why Evelyn had stopped upon entering the building. There would be no avoiding him. Stewart Dinklage from the mayor's office stood between them and the stairs leading to Casey's apartment.

He eyed them with a suspicious, penetrating stare, and his face and body twitched with small sudden jerks and spams. Adrian sensed Stewart's condition was self-afflicted, the result of misappropriating spiritual energy. It reminded him of some of the villagers he'd visited with Maruf, unwitting practitioners of dark magic, incurring injurious consequences for themselves instead of what they truly desired.

"Evelyn. How's your work with Hyde Properties going?" he asked, brushing the blonde hair from his forehead, side-glancing Adrian.

"It's going fine, Stewart... What are you doing here?"

"I've come to see Mr. Pincher. You remember him, right?" he said, unfurling his long fingers in her direction.

Evelyn held her breath to hide her disappointment. *With Terry upstairs, we can't reach Casey.*

Stewart clenched the muscles in his body, trying to dampen the shaking rippling up his spine, but the spasms were too powerful. Stewart writhed in his clothes, the bones of his shoulders and rib cage poking through his shirt.

Evelyn saw him very differently now than she had the first time they met. She considered charging past Stewart to Casey's apartment, then prying her friend away from Terry's clutches, but she knew better. Even if she succeeded, others would arrive before they could get away safely. Adrian stood beside her, ready for whatever course of action she preferred.

Instead of fighting Stewart, Evelyn decided to taunt him to see if she could find out what he really knew about Dyeworks. *By aggravating him, I can get him to tell us what we need to know.*

"I know who Terry is. I just didn't realize the mayor trusted you to have meetings on your own."

Stewart's eyes widened behind his glasses. "Everything happening here is because of me!" he snapped back at the offensive remark, clenching his fists.

"You're just an assistant. You're not in charge of development," she said, dismissing his contributions.

"I brokered the land!" Stewart screamed, spit spraying from his mouth. "I brought Ursula to Dyeworks!"

Stewart leaped forward with his arms outstretched, ready to choke Evelyn to death in his frustration, but Adrian grabbed him by the throat first. With one hand tightly clenched around his thin neck, he dragged Stewart away, punching him in the face repeatedly, bloodying his nose, and breaking his glasses. When Stewart's bony body crashed onto the ground, Adrian came forward and continued assaulting him, kicking him in the ribs several times.

Evelyn could not recognize Adrian through the rage. Stewart curled up in a ball on the floor, trying to protect himself, gasping for air. *He's going to kill him*, Evelyn realized.

"Adrian!" Evelyn screamed. "Stop! Please!"

She grabbed Adrian by the shoulders, trying to pull him away. He turned swiftly, with his clenched fist in the air, ready to fight. Evelyn braced for the hit, thinking the worst, but Adrian stopped and put his hands down. She looked deep into his eyes and saw so much emotion—fear, pain, shame, and profound confusion. *He's losing control.*

"Let's leave now," she said firmly to him.

With Stewart still cowering on the ground, Adrian followed Evelyn out of the lobby and back to the car. On the way back to her apartment, Evelyn worried for Adrian, who sat in the passenger seat beside her staring down at his knuckles. They were bruised and bloody, and he looked at them as if they were not his own.

As soon as Evelyn pulled onto her street, they realized that going to her apartment would be impossible. Even from a good distance, they could still see the group of men standing outside the entrance to the building—all people from her town. Given what they already knew and the break-in the night before, this was certainly no friendly welcome party.

"We can't be here," Evelyn said, turning the car around.

"I've been staying at the Riverside Inn," Adrian said. "No one knows who I am. We can spend the night there."

Given the circumstances, it was the best option they had. Evelyn had only ever gone there looking for Adrian, and she knew no one would expect to find her there. Once a colonial mansion, the inn sat atop a hill near the banks of Washisund River. From its location, one could see Dyeworks in the distance, as well as a couple of the other imposing industrial buildings upon the shore.

Majestic in its heyday, the inn now only catered to budget travelers, prostitutes, drunks, and junkies looking for discrete accommodation at an affordable price. Walking in through the door together, Adrian quickly took Evelyn across the faded red carpet of the reception hall, up the grand staircase, and down the wide corridor leading to room number four. He opened the door, and Evelyn saw it as if it were a photograph from a history book. The room looked like it had been last opened a century ago—a classic Victorian bedroom with custom woodwork and period detail, connected to a white-tiled bathroom, barely capable of fitting two persons at the same time.

Having been a guest of hers many times, Adrian felt suddenly ashamed that he did not have a more comfortable place to stay. The yellow wallpaper curled at its edges. A rusty radiator banged and sputtered beneath the window. A few pairs of shirts and pants hung in the closet, along with the one coat he'd worn the winter before, and several books were strewn over the flower-patterned bedspread.

"Please make yourself comfortable," he said, gesturing at the bed, the only place to sit in the room.

The floorboards creaked as Evelyn walked over. She pushed a couple of the books aside and sat down, causing the old wooden headboard to rattle against the wall. Adrian went to the other side and pushed the other books out of the way, forming a pile in the middle of the bed.

From the small window in the room, they could see the daylight fading. Without a plan of what to do next, Evelyn and Adrian decided to stay in the room for the remainder of the evening, discussing a potential plan. They put their feet up on the bed and looked at each other, comfortable in the knowledge that while the whole town was potentially looking for them, they were safe in each other's company.

"What did we learn?" Adrian asked, trying to make sense of the day.

"That James Wildes killed himself after his daughters' disappearances in 1802, and almost a century later, the town took his house away by eminent domain."

"And no other record exists for the property?"

"It's been under municipal control, so I don't see any transfers of ownership, not even the recent transaction with Hyde Properties."

"The factory has an unusual history and dark energies within, but we still do not know what we are dealing with."

"Stewart said *his family* knew about Dyeworks," Evelyn said, remembering something he had blurted out.

"Do you know who his family is?" Adrian asked, thinking maybe it was local knowledge.

"I have no idea. I just know him as the mayor's assistant."

"Then tomorrow, we will try to find out more about his family."

CHAPTER 11

URSULA AND TERRY walked up to Dyeworks at midnight with their black cloaks flapping in the cold breeze. Grant followed a few paces back, bewildered by their appearance. He turned his neck periodically to look at the growing group of people following closely behind, an odd mix from town. He'd been called to this strange meeting with only a promise from Ursula: "You will finally understand our secret tonight."

A dull quarter moon shined in the hazy sky, and the streetlamps buzzed and flickered as they entered the factory, stepping over rubble and passing through the hole in the exterior wall. The mayor, Analisa, and Fred walked in the middle of the procession of townspeople, among whom were Mr. Moulton, Herb Trentino, and the two female archivists from the public library. None of them stopped to question what they were doing or showed any signs of displeasure. Ursula summoned them, and they came, unquestioningly, to an abandoned building in the middle of the night.

Ursula and her team showed resolute determination in their eyes, but Grant's were filled with dubious concern. Everyone else stared blankly ahead, following the will of the dark energy that possessed them. Ursula came upon the edge of the hole and stopped, bowing her head in reverence, and the others gathered at the end of the long line of dye drums, close enough to see the deep cavity in the foundation. Ursula grinned as she invited Grant to step forward, holding her hand out to him. Beginning to look alarmed, he reluctantly stepped beside her.

"Why is everyone here tonight? What are you doing?" Grant demanded to know.

"Three projects we've done together. You must have wondered how things seem to go so well for us. Why Baneford's mayor is supporting us so enthusiastically," she said, pinching Mayor Jenkins' weathered cheeks. "You know as well as I do that money is not real power."

In the dim light of the factory, everyone watched the exchange with blank expressions, except for Terry, Fred, and Analisa, who already knew of what Ursula spoke.

"Why does everyone else have to be here for this conversation?"

"Because I require it, and they do as I ask," Ursula said. "I have a special power."

"And what's that?" Grant asked.

"I call on the power of ancient spirits. Come see."

Grant looked down into the hole with a sour expression. He could not see anything but the darkness at the bottom. He felt a hot wind against his face and heard distant sounds, chanting, and despairing voices calling out in an expanse. Grant sensed something other-worldly underneath his feet.

Ursula looked to Terry, and they smirked in agreement. They'd talked about this moment, how Grant would struggle with the truth. He was a realist who gave very little consideration to the idea of supernatural powers, divine, paranormal, or otherwise.

"Ancient spirits… Are you insane?" Grant roared, insulted about being mocked in this way.

The idea of standing there waiting for ghosts seemed ludicrous. Grant held back the desire to pull out of the deal right there to show Ursula he did not take kindly to people wasting his time. However, something in the back of his mind told him to hold on a little bit longer because the show was just about to begin, and supernatural forces would, in fact, emerge from the hole, reversing everything he believed to be true.

"I want to make this easy to understand for you, but the truth is not easy," Ursula said, removing a dagger from her inner robes with a handle of white bone.

"What's that?" he asked, wiping the hot sweat from his brow.

Several feet away, Mr. Moulton, Herb, the librarians, and the others watched the exchange between Ursula and Grant, placid and unmoved. Terry offered Grant looks of genuine sympathy.

"I will show you," Ursula said, extending her arm and slashing it with one swift move.

Grant flinched when the blood leaked from the cut, dripping off her arm into the darkness of the pit where he could not see. At once, the chanting he heard grew louder, emanating from the depths of the factory, "Shun-kah, Shun-kah, Shun-kah, Shun-kah." The words reverberated underground, and the townspeople joined in sync with the alien mantra, "Shun-kah, Shun-kah, Shun-kah." The air became electrified, and Grant's face turned white.

"Concentrated here, under Dyeworks, is an ancient power. The dead are the gatekeepers, and they require sacrifice," Ursula explained. "Now, I influence people and events according to my will. The weakest ones are offered, and the strongest join me on this journey," she added, gesturing to her team.

Terry, Fred, and Annalisa stepped away from the crowd and joined them at the precipice.

Under the light of dawn, Maruf sat in the open-air courtyard of his home, gazing out over the lush landscape, watching the world awaken. Word had come to him that a poor family in town believed their son to be possessed and desperately sought his counsel. As he'd done countless times before, Maruf agreed to meet with the boy and told the family to expect his visit. He arranged for a boat to take him to Aswan.

For this excursion, Maruf intended to travel alone because he believed the son's situation would not require hard work. In fact, Maruf did not expect to find signs of possession in the fifteen-year-old at all. It was how the family had described their son's current condition that convinced him. Those truly possessed were never "lethargic, meek, and withdrawn" for too long, as was said about the boy. Therefore, his malady was likely the result of something else—Maruf suspected some form of adolescent foolishness to be the cause. He opted to do the family the honor of visiting, even if it was a waste of time.

Later in the day, Maruf walked through the tall grass to the banks of the Nile. The boatsman ferried him through dark blue waters to Aswan, where he docked the boat and waited. Maruf stepped from the boat into a marketplace filled with merchant stalls, selling fruits, vegetables, seeds, spices, teas, and all sorts of valuable items. Old men roasted cobs of corn in the open plaza, children traded coins for sweets, and women carried baskets of bread on their heads, weaving through the crowds. Maruf passed at the edge of the scene, headed for the line of taxis at the other end of the market, and hired the first one to take him to the address where the family he was visiting lived.

They arrived at a bright blue, modest, mudbrick dwelling at the intersection of two dirt roads, Maruf knocked on the door, and two worried parents greeted him right away. They were weathered from a lifetime under the hot sun, meager in stature but overflowing with hospitality. They offered Maruf every drink and morsel of food in their home to honor his arrival, but he refused it all graciously, thanking them for their kindness. Behind them, in the corner, he saw the boy and went to him.

The boy lay on the bed on his back with his eyes shut. He was pale and breathed shallowly, his energy completely depleted. Maruf placed his hand on the young man's chest.

"Can you hear me?"

"Yes, I can," the boy croaked.

"And what is your name?"

"Omar," the boy whispered.

"He is not possessed," Maruf announced right away.

"Thank God!" the father cried.

Maruf circled the room, inspecting every wall. He looked at the parents, then the boy, then the parents again.

"I sense a dark energy here, but it is not possession. What do you believe is the cause of his malady?"

"He invited dark energy into this home!" the boy's mother confessed to Maruf, covering her eyes in shame. She went to the other side of the room and retrieved something from under the bed. It was a small earthen clay bowl. The mother returned with it to show Maruf and her husband what was inside—two gold coins with a sprinkle of dry blood spattered over them.

Maruf looked in the bowl, then returned his attention to the boy. He lifted the young man's hand, turning it to see the other side. He found a long, deep cut in the meat of his palm. It was a thick red line of raw, unhealed flesh where a scab should have already begun to form.

"He is practicing blood magic," Maruf said, holding the boy's hand up for the parents to see.

The mother wept and wailed, but the father kept quiet, wiping tears from his stony cheeks.

"What does he need so badly that he is willing to do this?" the father asked.

Maruf's eyes immediately traveled to the floor, thinking of what to say. He knew the answer and hoped not to say it for fear of embarrassing the poor parents. The boy had attempted to perform a very common ritual ill-informed practitioners believed created fortune. It was dark magic but an amateurish form, requiring merely a bit of one's own blood to invoke the magic. Due to its simplicity, it appealed to desperate people, unthinking of the consequences.

"He was trying to become wealthy," Maruf said, finally, unable to say what he really believed, that their son had practiced blood magic to acquire wealth because his family was poor. It was a plight for many of the youth in the poorer areas of the world, dreaming of better lives well out of reach.

Maruf explained to the family that, undisciplined and unpracticed, the boy had only managed to invite dark energy into his own body rather than conjuring any real magic, making him very weak as a result. He suggested a few days rest would fix him—provided he stopped meddling with such things immediately and forever. As he turned to leave, the parents kissed their hands and touched the top of their heads as a sign of gratitude and respect.

He feared their gratitude would be short-lived, however, as those curious enough to dabble with dark magic often dabbled more than once, seldom stopping after a single failed attempt. Maruf saw that the parents were quite ignorant of such matters, so he stopped to say what he needed to say clearly before walking out the door.

"Blood magic is the death of the soul."

With the trip even shorter than he'd predicted, Maruf took the taxi back to the market, then spent some time walking in and out of the stores and stalls, saying hello to old friends, and sharing cups of tea with new acquaintances. When he was ready to return home, Maruf made his way over to the dock. Looking over the water, he thought about what he had said to the family and how frightening it must have been to hear. The truth often was.

Many of the hauntings and possessions he'd encountered over the long years were the result of blood magic. The ancients used it profusely in their day, ultimately leading to their demise. Few knew as well as Maruf how it had dismantled Egypt's stability over millennia, how the world's first great civilization came to be buried and forgotten under the sand. Curses were more dangerous than snakes and scorpions in this land.

Maruf spotted the boatsman who'd brought him, waiting patiently onboard, and two foreign men standing by the water. Their appearance and clothing indicated they were not locals, yet he sensed something familiar about them. Approaching them to make his introduction, he caught a piece of their conversation in the Syrian dialect of Arabic.

"The voices were too loud to bear… making him mad… so he searched for a way out," the taller one said, stroking his black beard. "I am grateful for his good fortune."

"Praise God. He has gone home to his family," the other replied in affirmation.

Maruf came near. Dressed in a traditional galabia robe with a crown of gray hair, he appeared as a Nubian village elder.

"Peace be upon you," he said warmly. "My name is Maruf from the village of Seheil. It is my duty to welcome travelers to our home."

"And peace upon you," the taller one replied. "Please join us."

Maruf learned that the taller one's name was Nour. He had dark hair, a full beard, and thick, charcoal eyelashes like the Bedouins. His shorter friend, Sami, had a light complexion, blue eyes, and reddish hair. Though clearly not kin, they spoke and behaved in such a similar manner that Maruf surmised they'd been traveling companions for quite a long time. They did not carry items of great importance or value and were headed south for Sudan to engage in trade. He sensed they were honorable men about whom something was very different, so he asked a baited question that only a certain type of person could understand.

"What happens when the past is awakened?" He asked.

"The living world does not sleep," Nour answered naturally.

Maruf recognized they, too, were gifted men.

"We are kindred spirits. I invite you to come be my guests for a night or two before continuing with your journey."

"Thank you, brother. We are meeting an old friend here tonight," Nour said. "If your invitation extends to tomorrow, we would be happy to accept."

⁂

Ursula studied the crowd of townspeople that had gathered and wondered who the next sacrifice would be.

"A sacrifice will come forward for the Masters," she proclaimed.

The two librarians stepped aside, then the mayor, leaving Mr. Moulton standing alone. He stepped up with an apathetic demeanor, letting his toes dangle over the edge of the hole. Ursula grabbed Mr. Moulton by his hair and pulled him down, placing the blade against his neck. He barely twitched in protest, allowing the edge of the knife to press into the skin. Ursula swiftly ran the blade across his throat, slicing it open. Mr. Moulton lifted his hands to touch the blood spurting from his neck, and it leaked through his fingers onto his chest. Grant choked back the strong desire to vomit.

When Mr. Moulton's body was drained of life, it fell forward head-first into the hole. The top half of him disappeared into the darkness, but Grant could still see two legs sticking out, twisted against the inside wall of the hole. Then he heard movement below. Scattered pairs of tiny red hands gripped Mr. Moulton's legs. The creatures pulled themselves up, exposing their leathery faces to the dim light. They opened their jaws and gripped Mr. Moulton's flesh, ripping and chewing it apart.

"This is evil," Grant shouted at Ursula. "He had no idea what he was doing."

"The Masters only amplify what we already are. Don't you want to find out what you're capable of? Take part in the sacrifice, and you will feel them giving you strength. I want to give you this gift, but there is only one way."

Ursula licked Mr. Moulton's blood from the knife and handed it over to Grant. He knew what she wanted him to do. His hand shook as he held the knife, but he lifted it to his mouth and stuck out his tongue to taste the blood. Grant closed his eyes, and slowly, his hands stopped shaking. Ursula's words suddenly made sense.

Grant instantly recognized things were different. Somehow, the rules and limitations of the physical world had changed. The Masters would grant him the power to navigate, circumvent, and overcome any person or system presenting opposition to his interest. They offered it in exchange for his service to bring more blood for sacrifice. All empires were built on a foundation of blood.

Inside his own body, Grant also recognized something was different. He felt closely in tune with a more primal part of himself, fueling his emotions and giving him new strength. It coursed through his veins. His muscles told him he could leap from one end of the factory to the other or shatter someone's ribcage with a single strike. Words were insufficient to describe what it felt like to be invincible.

"Why are some affected more than others?" Grant asked Ursula.

"It has something to do with strength of character and purpose. Those with the weakest minds are influenced easily, and they're the ones we bring first."

"What do you mean first?"

"Not all sacrifices are willing. Those who are not susceptible to the influence require effort. But their value to the Masters is much greater, and so is our reward."

The goheiras devoured what remained of Mr. Moulton's body and returned into the depths, dragging his bones below. Ursula laughed loudly, bursting with ecstatic energy because she believed she knew who the Masters really wanted. It was obvious from the first moment the perfect sacrifice walked into the factory, an innocent lamb, ready for slaughter.

The day after he'd met the Syrians, Maruf went to the courtyard and looked out over the landscape, expecting to see his guests docking by the river and making their way through the tall grass to his home. It was hardly two minutes later that they arrived.

By the time they made it to the door of the house, the light in the sky had almost faded. Maruf wondered what he might learn from his guests during their short stay. Other than Adrian, it had been a long time since he'd come across others capable of accessing the spirit realm. When they stepped into his house, Maruf welcomed them in warmly. He showed them to their two private rooms, simple accommodations with only a bed inside, and allowed them time for some privacy and rest.

When they were well settled in, Nour and Sami joined him in the courtyard. Maruf brought loaves of whole wheat pita bread from the pantry and placed a large clay pot filled with okra and lamb stew to cook over the fire. They sat around the steaming cauldron savoring the rich aroma.

"Thank you, brother," Nour said. "We are very appreciative of your generosity."

"You honor your home and your country," Sami added.

By the time the stars shined brightly in the night sky, they were all at ease in each other's company, chatting comfortably. Maruf served the okra and lamb stew into their bowls, which they ate with the pita bread, tearing pieces to scoop it up. They filled their bellies and told each other ghostly tales to pass the time. Maruf recounted some of his most harrowing experiences, and they, in turn, shared theirs. These two Syrian men, he realized, were not amateurs in their craft nor inexperienced in their travels. He was particularly intrigued when they began speaking of their friend, Khalil. He was the third one in their fellowship, who'd gone missing one day without explanation. Nour and Sami assumed Khalil's curse had driven him mad.

Like Adrian, Khalil possessed the ability to commune with the dead and sense their pain. He, too, suffered greatly for having this gift. Unable to keep company with them any longer, he'd gone off looking for a remedy for his condition, wishing to shut himself off from the voices of the dead for fear of going mad. To Nour and Sami, Khalil's quest had seemed a search that would end up being in vain.

"He was always a very kind soul," Nour said.

"And his abilities were powerful," Sami added. "The spirits obeyed him because he felt their pain. I do not believe he ever truly realized the full extent of his power."

Maruf learned that Nour and Sami had traveled together since their small town of Maaloula in Syria had become a battleground for the ongoing bloody civil war. Not long after they'd left home, they met Khalil on the road, a young man from the heights in Lebanon, with no living family members remaining. Looking to use their gifts to make a living rather than end up dead themselves at the hands of religious fanatics and war-mongering idiots, men like Sami, Nour, and Khalil wandered through the region, traveling from place to place, visiting with whoever asked for their assistance. News of their abilities traveled quickly, and fortunately, they were not without work for long. Like Adrian, they charged a fee for their services when appropriate, and compensation was neither steady nor consistent. However, occasionally, wealthy persons expressed their gratitude with large sums, and the economics fared better over the long term.

Even though Nour and Sami were not blood, the depth of their bond was unmistakable. Sleeping in the same rooms, eating every meal with the other, praying shoulder to shoulder, and dispelling spirits together, they'd taken on the same mannerisms, facial expressions, and colloquialisms. They were generous, considerate, and self-sacrificing for one another. Maruf imagined it had been the same with Khalil, too.

"But he was tormented," Nour said of Khalil. "All he wanted was to be free. The voices grew so loud we feared he might tear his own head open... That's when he left. We were surprised to receive a message from him last month asking us to meet him in Aswan by the dock. It had been two years since we'd heard his news. The friend we were waiting for yesterday when you invited us to your home was Khalil."

"Did he find what he was looking for?" Maruf asked. He hoped that Khalil's story might help Adrian in some way. "My friend is also cursed."

Nour sat back and stroked his black beard, deliberating the best way to answer.

"Some people have in them an inner vulnerability. A broken heart. It bleeds for everyone—especially the weeping spirits. Khalil was this way—easily affected by their emotions. It opens a way for the dead to control a man."

Sami nodded in agreement. Maruf knew Adrian was this way, too. By way of his empathetic heart, he left himself open, and the dead came to impose. He allowed himself to feel their pain, and they accepted the invitation.

"When we saw Khalil yesterday, he gave us this," Sami said, removing a rolled parchment from his robes. He opened it, and Maruf saw the lettering at the top was in old Aramaic. The scroll contained the image of a circle divided into three equal parts. In each section, words and symbols filled the negative space, depicting some type of ritual.

"This is how Khalil freed himself from their voices. The ritual provides protection so the dead cannot enter without invitation. It is a ritual with three parts, but it requires a person to both love and be loved by another. To perform it, three distinct actions must be taken: Declare a love, risk one's life for another, and finally, accept love in return. Three actions undertaken with sincerity and purpose."

"My friend already loves a woman, and he has risked his life for her many times," Maruf said, throwing another log on the fire. "Why should this be any different?"

"Because it is she that must perform the ritual. When we met Khalil yesterday, he was with his wife. She was the one who set him free. The curse is only undone by the love of another," Sami said, giving Maruf the parchment. "Khalil gave it to us. I believe it was meant for you or perhaps your friend. You know as well as we do there is no such thing as coincidence."

Maruf held the parchment in his hands and looked at the ritual's three parts. It was an innocent form of magic, the channeling of one's love to provide protection. He'd only heard about Evelyn from Adrian. Maruf wondered if she'd be the one to save Adrian from his curse if she could sincerely carry out the three parts.

"I thank you for this gift," Maruf said to his guests. "I am grateful that you accepted my invitation."

Growing tired and sleepy by the fire, Nour and Sami eventually retired to their rooms. Maruf stayed in the courtyard, under the night sky, deep in thought. He'd have to wait for Adrian to return to Egypt to share news of the parchment. Eventually, he hoped, Adrian would find the same peace that Khali's wife had afforded him.

CHAPTER 12

ADRIAN AND EVELYN ventured out of the Riverside Inn late morning and picked up breakfast sandwiches at a nearby drive-thru. Evelyn needed to search the internet to find out more about Stewart's family; however, fleeing her apartment the night before, she left her cell phone. Now, she was willing to tempt fate and enter her apartment one last time to retrieve her phone and use the computer.

"I can use my computer, get my phone, and grab anything else we may need," she said between bites of egg and cheese. "It's not like they're going to wait outside forever."

Adrian reluctantly agreed. They found Mox Street quiet, no one standing outside, and no faces pressed against the windows in the apartment above. A brisk walk from the car to the entrance, and they were safe and out of sight. Evelyn showered and changed her clothes. She emerged from her bedroom with wet hair, a fresh shirt, a pair of jeans, and a black carry bag in her hand.

At the computer, she looked for any information she could find on Stewart Dinklage, accessing the same sites she used as an agent to search for delinquent property owners. Public records suggested Stewart was a private person. Born to Henry and Abigail Dinklage, Stewart did not use social media or leave behind any kind of searchable web activity. The records indicated he'd been a student at Old Bedford high, graduated from Boston College with a bachelor's in political science, and was never married. The most recently dated file, stamped shortly after his graduation, mentioned Stewart's appointment as assistant to the mayor. Evelyn knew he was already involved with Mayor Jenkins' reelection campaign.

Going deeper, Evelyn accessed property records. She found Stewart owned his home in Baneford, quite close to where Casey lived. He'd inherited the home from his mother, Abigail Wildes.

"His mother is called Wildes?" Adrian asked, perking up.

"She changed her name after she got married. The transfer of ownership on Stewart's house used her maiden name because that's how it was first recorded."

"We should speak with Stewart again."

Remembering how things had gone with Stewart last time, Evelyn feared Adrian losing his temper again, but the possibility of finding out the true story of Dyeworks seemed too compelling to ignore. According to the property records, Stewart lived at 81 Millbrook Street, a single-family home nestled in a quiet residential area. It was a steeply pitched two-story Tudor with a brick stucco façade, a style of house less common in Baneford. They could not see into the house because all the curtains on the first floor were drawn. With the garage door closed, they worried he might not be home.

They waited in Evelyn's car for about twenty minutes, scanning the scene to see if anyone came or went before attempting to enter themselves. Adrian led Evelyn along the narrow walkway to the back of the house and peered through the kitchen window. Looking past the kitchen and the open dining room, they saw Stewart sitting on the living room couch, flipping through a stack of documents on his lap.

Finding the back door to the kitchen unlatched, Adrian took Evelyn's hand and led her into the house. They tiptoed quietly out of the kitchen and into the hallway that would lead them to Stewart undetected. Evelyn saw no decorations or personal effects in the home, no paintings hanging on the walls, not even a single photo in a frame. *What a miserable life*, she thought as they paused outside the living room for a moment before pouncing on Stewart.

He recoiled as soon as they entered the room, still reeling from the recent beating. Stewart instinctually turned his bruised face away and covered his ribs. Adrian held Stewart down firmly, pressing him into the couch with both arms, refraining from causing any real pain.

"We just want to talk," Evelyn said, trying to assuage some of Stewart's fear. He shot back an expression of palpable disgust through bruised and swollen eyes, heavy breathing, and spasms under Adrian's hold.

"What do you want?" he barked.

"For you to answer our questions," Adrian said, staring him down. Adrian let go, and Stewart shrank. He pushed his glasses up his bruised nose and sat up. Adrian and Evelyn took the two chairs opposite him.

"We've seen the sacrifices, those hideous creatures, and we know people are under some kind of spell. Tell us, what is Ursula looking for at Dyeworks?" Evelyn demanded.

"Power," he said, exhaling deeply. "It doesn't matter what you've seen if you don't know what you're looking at."

"How is it that you have come to understand these things?" Adrian asked, speaking in a stern tone of voice. "Passed down in your family, perhaps?" Stewart looked at them mischievously, and they saw his confidence grow just thinking of it.

"Fifteen generations! That's how far it had to travel to reach me."

"James Wildes was your relative," Evelyn said, affirming their theory.

"But it was my great aunt Sarah that received the gift."

Adrian looked closely at Stewart. He sensed the spasms in his body were manifestations of a curse, unfolding slowly, no doubt brought about by his involvement with dark forces. A scrawny young man, Stewart resembled a wet chick more than a man.

"When did you start to shake?" Adrian asked aggressively.

"I don't know what you're talking about," Stewart stammered. His hands trembled only slightly, but the involuntary tremors causing his body to jerk in unnatural ways were impossible to miss.

"Why did this power come to Sarah Wildes?" Evelyn asked. "Why was she chosen?"

"Because of her pain. The Wildes sisters would've been better off not having a father. There's no way to know how many times he raped them, but I do know Sarah was the oldest. That's years of extra pain and cruelty she endured. Her mother was already gone, but Annawan saw her pain."

"Who?" Evelyn asked. Adrian knew it was the native man from his vision.

"He was an Algonquin leader once, a chief, who lost his wife and young daughter to fever. Naturally, he blamed the white man for bringing disease to his shores. Legend says he searched endlessly for a way to see his family again. Instead, he came upon an ancient power buried in the ground. And it was located underneath James Wildes' house. When Annawan saw the depth of Sarah's pain, reminding him of his own, he could not keep the power for himself." A spasm shook Stewart's body, wiggling through his neck, causing him to make horrendous faces. "Annawan came across Sarah walking in the woods alone, and he gave her a knife with a bone handle," Stewart continued. "He told her that all her desires could be fulfilled through sacrifice. Later that same night, she lured her sisters outside and slit their throats."

"And James Wildes?" Evelyn asked.

"Sarah saw her wish granted when she found her father hanging in the barn from a noose he'd fashioned himself. The Masters gave Sarah true power over this world, and she controlled Baneford for the rest of her days. Few people learned the truth, but whispers became legends."

"And that knife that Annawan gave to Sarah," Adrian said, "it belonged to you. Now it belongs to someone else."

"What does Ursula and Hyde Properties have to do with this?"

"Because I didn't have millions of fucking dollars to buy the factory myself!" Stewart snapped at Evelyn.

"So, you gave away your birthright?"

"I brought the Masters exactly what they wanted!"

"But it wasn't you. It was Ursula," Evelyn said.

"That is the reason for this condition," Adrian warned. "The Masters have cursed you for being a coward."

"We've already started the sacrifices," Stewart replied with a shaky voice. "I was there for two of them. I'm a part of this as much as anyone, but Ursula was the one who had the money to buy the building. She had the team. And she's followed the Masters for a very long time."

"There are followers?" Evelyn asked.

"There are pockets of energy buried all throughout New England, remnants of a long-forgotten time when our ancestors wielded great power. They belong to the Masters, and there are many who revere them. Ursula is one of those. She knew what needed to be done."

"It is a shame that you call these evil spirits 'Masters.' You would not revere them if you knew what they truly are." Adrian knew that what Stewart spoke of was the worst form of magic there was—the sacrificing of innocent lives for power. Regardless of where the Masters came from or what they were capable of, he could not look past the very simple fact that they were evil. He cringed to think what sorts of horrors people who thought this way could inflict upon the world.

A convulsion shot through Stewart's body, and for a moment, he looked like he might vomit. Clenching his thighs with his long fingers, Stewart willed his body to stop shaking.

"How did the town end up owning the house?" Evelyn asked.

"Eventually, the town took the house by eminent domain, thinking they could stop my family from accessing the power. It stayed under municipal control until I came to office. All the mayor wanted was money. Now it's ours, and we're just getting started. Given enough time, you'll break too, just like everyone else."

Evelyn saw the rage in Adrian's eyes. Before she could say anything, he had his hands around Stewart's throat, squeezing, trying to end his life. She stood up and pulled hard at Adrian, trying to pry him away, and it took all her strength to get him off, shouting at his back.

"Stop! We're leaving now!"

Adrian turned and stared back at her, shaken by how little control he had over himself. He hadn't meant to do that, and this wasn't the first time. Wanting to leave, Evelyn walked out, and Adrian followed, giving Stewart a final vicious glance before heading out the door.

When she got in the car, Evelyn's inclination was to go to a place she and Adrian knew well, where they could be alone. She cut across town and took Pennyworth Road straight to Echo Lake. They gained in elevation as the car circled the lake, coming from the top of the foothills to the base. A picturesque scene of the water emerged, glistening under the midday sun. Evelyn led Adrian to the lakeshore, where they'd nearly died fighting Hendrick just over three months ago.

Around the lake, a series of granite boulders sat at the edge of the water. Evelyn walked to one and found a groove in the rock worthy of being a seat. She hopped onto it and patted the space beside her, signaling for Adrian to join.

"Are you okay?" she asked, genuinely concerned about his state of mind.

"If our fight truly is against people, then I fear sooner or later, someone will have to die," he said with a solemn tone. Though his work was with the dead, Adrian had never killed anyone before, and it was not something he wished to do.

"It's Ursula we should be pursuing. Maybe if we stop her, no one else has to die," Evelyn said.

Only a few pedestrians walked along the shore, dressed in tracksuits with headphones on. Evelyn hoped that being here would remind Adrian of himself. She knew it was an awful thing to consider killing a person. Evelyn desperately hoped it would not come to that. They remained there for a few hours, staring out over the shimmering lake, breathing the crisp spring air, and finding peace in the silence.

"I'd like to go to Casey's one more time... just in case she's there alone. Do you think that's okay?" Evelyn asked, nervous to be turned down.

"It is risky. If we see anyone outside, we will not be able to enter," Adrian warned. "But we can try..."

With the town becoming increasingly dangerous, Evelyn wished she could reach her best friend and tell her the truth about what was going on. On the way over in the car, she was grateful for how willing Adrian was to risk his life for others. On Casey's street, they observed no suspicious activity and no one standing in the vacant lobby. Adrian accompanied Evelyn into the building, and they went up three flights of stairs to Casey's apartment. Evelyn knocked loudly on the door. When no one came, Adrian turned the knob and found the door unlocked. Walking inside, they were struck by the mess all around.

Clothes and odd items were strewn over the floor in many of the rooms. Pots and pans were piled up in the kitchen sink, wet towels were bunched up in the bathroom by the tub, and the apartment smelled of stale air and ripening trash. Sweeping through, Evelyn confirmed Casey was not there. By the looks of things, she was not as well as she seemed.

"I'm so scared for you," Evelyn whispered into the empty space.

Adrian peered out the window blinds in the living room, then the bedroom, checking the street outside, concerned about being in the apartment too long. That's when the two intruders came crashing through the front door. The first was a gigantic man, almost as tall as the ceiling, and when he proceeded into the hallway, his shoulders touched the wall on both sides. Evelyn saw that it was Bob Seward.

Adrian stepped into the hallway, and Bob lurched forward with his meaty fists clenched. Sliding through the narrow space, he plowed into Adrian, knocking him back, falling on top of him, and knocking the wind from his lungs. Bob hit him in the face repeatedly with his giant paws, bloodying his nose. Adrian used all his strength to wrestle away, having no advantage on the floor.

He stood up, blood dripping down his chin, and attacked Bob, punching from a distance, using his long reach to avoid being pulled under the suffocating weight. Bob retreated backward, and when he passed across the doorway a second time, Evelyn smashed his head with the base of Casey's table lamp. His body collapsed under the archway onto the floor, shaking the apartment.

Evelyn took a wide step over Bob and into the hallway, where she saw Ed Crowley by the door. His uniform was tattered and untucked, the puss-festering wounds on his bald head oozed and bled. He held a vacant stare in his eyes and pulled his gun from its holster.

Adrian shoved Evelyn back into the living room and down onto the floor just as Ed began shooting into the apartment. Lying face down on the hardwood, they heard his footsteps edging closer. Positioning himself by the door, Adrian grabbed the barrel of the gun the second he saw it and ripped the weapon away from Ed.

Adrian turned the gun around in his hand and hammered Ed over the head, pistol-whipping him with the stock end of his Smith & Wesson. Ed fell to his knees, and Adrian continued beating him. Evelyn tried to pry the gun away, but Adrian shoved her to the side, blind with rage. Desperate to make him stop, she slapped him across the face as hard as she could, screaming, "You're killing him!"

He paused to look down at the bloody gun handle in his hands.

"Go!" she screamed.

Evelyn pushed Adrian into the hallway and forced him out of the apartment. He walked away with his head hanging low, like a boy freshly disciplined by his mother. She knew better than to admonish him because he was clearly losing control. As she turned the key to start her car, it hit Evelyn just how dangerous Adrian's condition was. She steered her car back to the one place they had left to go in town, the Riverside Inn.

Avoiding eye contact with the young receptionist in the lobby, Evelyn and Adrian went up the grand staircase, returning to his room. Evelyn slapped his face the second the door was shut. He took the hit, unflinching like he deserved it. But Evelyn wasn't mad at him for losing control; she just needed a way to let the anger out. She kissed him because it was the only thing left to do.

She leaned into him with her body and put her lips on his. Immediately, Adrian's demeanor changed. His shoulders shifted back, and he cupped Evelyn's face in his hands, returning the kiss. He took a deep breath into his diaphragm and took the weight of the world off his back long enough to feel the joy. He'd thought about her every day for months, longed for the taste and smell of her, and now, finally, that moment had come.

Adrian removed Evelyn's clothes and admired her skin from head to toe like a parched man gazing upon water in a desert oasis. Even under the unforgiving light of a solitary bulb hanging over the bed, the sight of her alone revived Adrian's spirit. He ran his fingers through her hair and down her back, stopping at the curves of her hips. She unbuttoned his jeans and lifted his shirt over his head.

Naked together at the Riverside Inn, in a room forgotten by time, Adrian and Evelyn were never more aware of how important it was to live in the present. Separate from ancient curses and promises of a better future, the here and now offered them everything they needed. Adrian did not say the words, "I love you," but he let her see it in every glance and feel it in every caress from his hands. Evelyn saw the man she loved before, filled with passion and the determination to win.

Evelyn gave herself to Adrian entirely, letting go of yesterday's trivialities. He'd left without saying a word, but he came back. He did not say what she wished to hear, but he risked his life for her every chance there was. She welcomed him into her body, and it was right like it had never been with anyone else. The headboard banged against the wall, their breaths quickened, pleasure mounted, and at the very core of the act, a profound love expressed itself.

That night, they slept without a stitch of clothing on their bodies, nestled closely together under the covers. The radiator rattled, the ceiling creaked under the footsteps of inn guests roaming above, and the bed was neither spacious nor comfortable, but it felt like home. Adrian fell asleep first, leaving Evelyn awake alone with a mind to wander. Listening to his breathing, she wished for a way to save him from the worst yet to come.

Adrian had said it first; "someone would have to die." Evelyn didn't want him to die, and she didn't want him to bloody his hands either and bear the weight of murder on his conscience alone. Given his recent outbursts, Adrian needed to be shielded from harm, not pushed into it. Evelyn thought of a way to stop Ursula, and it called for seeing Mayor Jenkins again. Given the risks, she decided to go alone.

CHAPTER 13

THE NEXT MORNING, when Adrian was in the shower, Evelyn walked out of the inn, got in her car, and drove straight to the mayor's office. She told herself the situation called for bravery and that if she could accomplish the task alone, the risk was worth taking to avoid putting Adrian in a position where he might lose control. The mayor had the power to stop the development, blocking access to the site, so she'd have to disturb the lion's den.

When she arrived, the pristineness of the neighborhood betrayed the truth of the situation. The white neoclassical building shined in the sunlight at the center of its perfectly landscaped grounds. Evelyn imagined it would be hard to convince anyone that that town was cursed with an evil spell because, from where she stood, nothing looked amiss. After checking in with security, Evelyn marched across the lobby, went up to the second floor, crossed the carpeted reception room, and came upon the mayor's office door. She took a deep breath before pushing it open and going inside.

She saw Mayor Jenkins, Stewart, Chief Rawlings, attorneys Horowitz and Brown, and zoning council delegates Bill Oates and Denise Sheeran seated around the mayor's desk. They looked up at her with morbid fascination, each in their own peculiar manner, breathing madness into the air.

"I hope you don't mind me joining you," she said nonchalantly.

They continued to look at her with bewilderment, except Stewart, who turned purple with rage. Bruised and bandaged but no longer alone, he protested her presence in the office.

"She can't be in here!" he whined.

"Why not?" Chief Rawlings barked back, licking the donut frosting from his fingertips.

"Look what they did to me!" Stewart shouted out of his bruised and swollen face.

"You can sue her for assault," Horowitz advised Stewart, keeping Evelyn in the corner of his eye.

"And trespassing," Brown added, squinting his eyes at Evelyn from behind his thick lenses. "Was she the one who did this to you?"

The mayor looked around the room at all the faces, then back at Evelyn. His face was tense, and he breathed heavily through his mouth. "I don't care about her! What's the next agenda item we need to push through?" Mayor Jenkins yelled, turning toward Oates and Sheeran.

Oates stood up to speak, his gray comb-over floating over the room. "The demo permits. They've already started, so we backdated them," he said out of his plump face. "Sign, and we're good to go."

Seated next to him, Sheeran pulled a document from the manilla folder on her lap and placed it on the mayor's desk. Evelyn struggled to believe they were so brazen to forge official documents in view of a crowd, but the mayor signed it immediately without question.

"Good!" the mayor said, sliding the document back to Oates' frumpy colleague with dry hair.

Sheeran picked it up and examined the signature from behind her thick red glasses before putting it back in the folder.

"We also need something for the clerk's office," Sheeran added. "Identification and copies of licensure for all contractors assigned by Hyde properties."

"Shut up, Denise!" Oates barked at her. "I told you, I'll take care of that."

"That constitutes negligence on the part of the town for not disclosing requirements earlier in the process," Horowitz interrupted. "The town should sue the town!"

Chief Rawlings, barely listening, picked up another donut from the box on the table. He put his mouth on its side and sucked the jelly from the center, getting powdered sugar in his mustache and nose in the process.

They're all nuts, Evelyn thought to herself. Watching the insanity unfold, she could not determine if it was the overly litigious attorneys, corrupt officials, or Stewart's discolored face that bothered her the most.

"Ursula would not want her to be here!" Stewart shouted again, stomping his foot loudly on the hardwood floor. They all froze to contemplate what he said—Ursula's name struck fear in them.

"Tie her up then!" Chief Rawlings grumbled, with the mayor nodding frantically in agreement.

Evelyn did not fight Horowitz or Brown when they restrained her, recognizing her plan had already gone awry. Sheeran moved fast to fetch the duct tape they used to bind her hands behind her back. Stewart delighted at the sight of it, while neither Oates nor the mayor saw any problem with two attorneys restraining a woman in the mayor's office without just cause as the chief of police sat and watched. They pushed Evelyn into a seat in the corner of the room while Stewart sent the message informing Ursula of her presence.

For the next two hours, Stewart looked intermittently over at Evelyn, reprimanding her with his gaze, while the others seemed to forget entirely that she was there. Enmeshed in their loud and irrational exchanges, they put her out of mind, and she blended into the surroundings of the room. Evelyn quietly observed the madness, hearing some of the ways they were cutting corners at Dyeworks. Greed and unwavering loyalty to Ursula influencing their actions.

Stewart quivered in his seat when Ursula and Grant walked through the door. They observed the group sitting around the mayor's desk, then turned to look at Evelyn sitting with her hands tied in the corner. Neither of them expressed surprise or concern about seeing her that way, and Evelyn understood the time for lying was over.

"Her will is strong," Ursula whispered to Grant, the long strands of her black hair brushing against the fabric of his suit.

Grant continued staring at Evelyn, trying to understand whatever it was that made her special. She stared back at him, looking past the gold cufflinks and perfectly tailored clothes, to discover he was no longer inside. There was a new vacantness in his stare that she recognized, having seen it in others around town. *Ursula's influence doesn't affect me*, Evelyn realized. *I'm the outlier.*

"We both said you were special the day we met you," Ursula said. "Although maybe having different reasons," she added, chuckling. "It turns out we were right... I'd like to ask Stewart to kindly escort you outside to the car."

"Where are we going?" Evelyn asked, seeing Stewart get up to come her way.

"A party," Ursula said, causing Grant to smile.

Stewart removed the duct tape from Evelyn's wrists, grabbed her securely by the arm, and escorted her from the office, following them down to the limousine in the underground garage. Once inside, the car took a familiar route towards Old Bedford, and Evelyn saw they were headed to Grant's house. She grimaced from the memory of being there last and wondered for the first time if Ursula's spell had influenced her behavior that night. *If it affected me then, why doesn't it affect me now?* Evelyn asked herself. The only thing she could think of that changed after that night was Adrian's return.

For such a short ride, it was quite awkward, with Ursula and Grant sitting across from Evelyn, displaying the faces of two disapproving parents.

"She knows," Stewart mouthed to Ursula, twitching and crackling his knuckles.

"Because you told her!" Ursula snapped at him. "But it doesn't matter... she's with us now," she added, keeping her eyes fixed on Evelyn the rest of the drive.

They took the elevator up to the living room where they were soon joined by Casey and Terry. Ursula greeted them warmly, Grant disappeared into one of the other rooms in the house, and Stewart stayed close by Evelyn's side, keeping watch.

"They've broken through. We meet the Masters tonight," Ursula said to Terry, her eyes wet with emotion, but it was Casey who responded first.

"I can't wait," she said emphatically. It frightened Evelyn that Casey was now in their fold and would not look in her direction.

"It's because of your faith that we're here," Terry said as a good disciple would.

Grant returned and pointed everyone's attention to the chilled champagne on the console table. With cause for celebration, they poured their glasses, toasted, shared gratitude, and even included Stewart in the merriment.

Hearing their talk of meeting the Masters, Evelyn expected a return to Dyeworks after nightfall and feared what awaited them there this evening. She thought of ways of escaping or simply running out the door, but she knew she wouldn't get far. Even if she did, in the end, there was nowhere to go in Baneford that was safe. Evelyn would have to start a new life somewhere else or accept the reality here, and this was home.

With Ursula right there, Evelyn recognized this was as good an opportunity as any to find out more about who she was and her strange religion. Mustering the courage to draw attention back onto herself, she confronted Ursula.

"I thought you were here to develop Dyeworks and make a difference in our town," Evelyn started in an accusatory tone. "You lied to me."

"We're going to do everything we promised to do and more," Ursula replied, shaking her head to dismiss Evelyn's error.

"Why should anyone trust you after what you've done?"

A silence ensued, and Evelyn felt all the eyes in the room upon her, sizing up the gravity of the offense.

"Because I know the Masters, and you don't," Ursula replied, speaking in a calm tone. "In my office several weeks ago, I told you how I built my company and where I came from. But I never told you what I found at that first property I bought with my husband. Buried under the foundation was a tiny room, sealed in the earth. I thought we'd found an ancient burial site, but when we entered inside, only I heard the voices. The Masters have guided me for many years."

"Who are they, and why do you believe in them?" Evelyn demanded to know.

"The Masters were sorcerers, living thousands of years before the first civilizations are said to have existed," Ursula explained, her tone earnest with devotion. "They lived here, in this corner of the world, wielding unimaginable power.

You asked how I can promise Dyeworks will be built... because I have access to *that* power."

"How?"

"The second time I went into that small room alone, the Masters spoke to me again. They showed me a vision of what I could be. I saw a person who was strong, successful, and safe from ever being hurt or abused the way I was as a child. The Masters offered me a way to save my own life, and I took it. I probably felt the way you do now. I didn't want to sacrifice my husband... he wasn't a bad man, but he was quite simple-minded. When I let him go, I became so much more than I ever imagined possible. I received what the Masters had promised."

"What about you?" Evelyn screamed at Grant, Terry, and Stewart. "You're okay with killing people? What you're doing is evil!"

"Be quiet!" Stewart barked back.

"I've worked with Ursula for three years, and I believe in the work she's doing," Terry interjected. "Consider the good she's done for your friend," he added, inviting Casey to step up and give her testimony.

"Evie, remember how unhappy I was before I met Terry?" I don't feel that way anymore, and I'm not scared to live my life. Terry says it's because of Ursula's magic. I'm happy... isn't that what you wanted for me?"

"Yes, but I didn't want you involved with an evil cult!" Evelyn pleaded in futility.

"Evil is a matter of perspective," Grant interrupted. "The ocean drowns people every year, but it's not inherently bad. Sailing over it, people created new life and opportunities."

"You can't control evil," she said to deaf ears.

When it was time to leave, Ursula and Terry donned their black cloaks. The boisterous celebration from before was replaced by a solemn silence as they descended in the elevator and piled into the two cars that would take them back to Dyeworks.

Immediately after nightfall, Ursula led them around the factory to the back of the building, where the crew had opened the exterior wall. They stepped over the rubble and entered the factory, walking right up to the hole in the foundation. Evelyn gasped when she saw how much larger it was. Somehow, the pit had expanded considerably, with the top widening and the depth of the crater reaching further down into the ground. With just enough light shining on the bottom of the hole, Evelyn saw an entrance to a tunnel. It appeared tall enough for a person to pass through.

The faint moonlight began to draw faces out of the dark, townspeople slowly filtering in. They amassed at the other end of the broad pit. Evelyn recognized many of them, cringing at the extent of Ursula's spell. Trevor, Cam, Ed, the mayor, and countless others stood staring across the hole, entranced. Ursula turned to address the crowd.

"The Masters are waiting!" she announced. "Tonight, we will honor them!"

The sound of chanting slowly filled the hall, like a low-frequency hum. It emanated from the hole first before the townspeople joined in, keeping in sync with the ominous calls.

"Shun-kah…Shun-kah…Shun-kah."

Evelyn saw movement. Two goheiras scaled out of the hole, clutching the side walls with their hands and feet to prop their hideous faces over the edge. Further down, she spotted something else. In the space no larger than a bedroom, dozens more goheiras stood, packed tightly together in perfectly formed rows, extending beyond the hole and into the tunnel. From above, they appeared as a single mass of deformed gra   y and crimson flesh, swelling with anticipation.

"Who steps forward tonight?" Ursula asked of the crowd.

Two young men Evelyn did not know stepped forward, holding Ed Crowley securely between them. He had black circles under his eyes, bruises on his cheekbones, tattered clothes, and very little of himself remaining. Analisa and Fred lit wooden torches and held them high, blazing over their heads. The light shined on Ed, and Evelyn saw the boils on his scalp had spread with infection. They connected in a single sprawling puss-filled wound at the crown of his head. He shuffled forward, and Ursula greeted him by placing her hand on his shoulder.

Ursula took Ed's arm and extended it over the pit, pulling the knife from her robes. She sliced his wrist with a single swift gesture, and dark blood spilled out, dripping onto the two goheiras at her feet and the backs of the ones below. The goheiras clicked and stomped their feet so hard that the hall shook, and the two at the top descended back down, disinterested in the sacrifice.

Ed did not scream or try to run. He simply stared at his wrist with an exasperated look in his eyes, watching the blood leak profusely down his forearm. It collected in the sleeve of his tattered police uniform and continued to drip into the hole, splattering over the goheiras' wrinkled faces. They abruptly turned their backs away from Ursula, showing their disapproval.

"Don't you control them?" Evelyn asked.

"They belong to the Masters," Ursula replied.

"Well, they don't want Ed, so leave him alone."

Ursula locked eyes with Evelyn as she launched her foot into Ed's gut. He doubled over and fell backward into the hole. In an instant, the goheiras cleared out of the way, forcing Ed's body to crash hard onto the dirt. He landed chest down at the center of the goheiras and did not move. Evelyn believed he might be dead.

"Why don't they want him?" Terry asked, staring down into the pit.

Instead of eating Ed, the goheiras curled their lips back, revealing rows of needle-pointed spikes. With their jaws clenched shut, they spit a clear liquid through their teeth, spritzing Ed with their slimy saliva. Thoroughly soaked, he began to slip and slide on the floor, struggling to stand. The goheiras formed a wide circle around him, and Fred let his torch fall over Ed's head. He was on fire instantly from their virulent spit. Evelyn screamed as she watched Ed Crowley burn to death, shuddering on the ground, the stench of his smoldering flesh filling the air.

When the flames died down, all that was left of him was a pile of charred remains, which the goheiras refused as well.

"That's not who they want," Analisa said, looking up at Ursula.

"Who do they want?" Grant asked, testing her.

"His spirit was weak.... easily influenced. The Masters will reward us if we honor them with the right ones. Almost anyone is worth more than that dumb cop," Ursula said.

Evelyn hated to hear them speak ill of Ed, with his body still smoldering. Disgusted by how little regard they had for human life, she wished she could punch each of them in the face, but instead, she directed her aggression verbally at Ursula.

"You clearly have no idea what you're doing because you're evil and fucking crazy!"

"It won't matter what you think much longer. Only blood pays for life, and apparently, yours is special."

Grant's eyes grew larger when he understood that Ursula intended to sacrifice Evelyn. She'd shown remarkable resilience to the Masters' influence.

"You're going to offer *her*?" Grant asked Ursula with alarm in his voice.

"Not yet. But if you have a problem with it, you can take her place."

"Get rid of her already!" Stewart shouted, shuffling forward with irritation.

Ursula's face turned sour. She grabbed Stewart by his shirt color, dragging him on his feet, flinging his wiry frame into the hole. He landed on a pile of Ed's smoldering bones and ashes, surrounded by dozens of goheiras and screaming in terror.

"You're a coward," Ursula yelled down into the hole.

Stewart's screams turned to pitiful moans, but he fought against the aches and spasms in his body and stood up. The goheiras turned their backs at once, facing the other direction, hissing loudly.

"They don't want him either?" Terry said.

"They don't want me," he shouted back up at them. "My family has honored them for generations, remember? They have my blood. Rebecca and Susanna Wildes. Give them someone they want." Stewart looked into the mysterious tunnel leading out from the bottom of the hole, trying to see the other end. Preventing him from going any further, the red beasts amassed at the entrance, blocking the way. Some of them snapped their jaws at Stewart, warding him off.

"Get me out of here!" Stewart pleaded.

Ursula ignored the request and grabbed Evelyn's arm, pulling her close. With a grip like a vice, Ursula straightened Evelyn's arm over the pit and used the knife to cut her and make the blood flow. It dripped onto the creatures' faces below, and they licked it, smacking their lips and making clicking sounds with intermittent squeals of delight. The goheiras parted around the entrance of the tunnel and stood aside, inviting Ursula and her followers to come down.

"They want more," Terry said.

"Come." Ursula went down first, sliding comfortably against the dirt wall all the way to the bottom.

Fred and Annalisa pushed Evelyn to the edge and slowly lowered her in. She grasped at the dirt walls, holding anything she could find to climb down without falling. The townspeople watched as the rest of them piled in, the mayor and chief of police content to wait in the dark with everyone else.

As they came down, the goheiras emptied out from the landing area, heading into the tunnel dug out of the rock. Standing across from it now, Evelyn saw how the tunnel traveled straight under the foundation while another, smaller tunnel beside it deviated downward, heading into the unknown depths.

Annalisa relit her torch and led the way, creating light in the dark passageway. Ursula followed right behind her, eager to get to the other side and see what the Masters had waiting for her. Walking comfortably with enough height in the tunnel, they proceeded about twenty feet under the factory floor and came upon a chamber. It was a rectangular room with high ceilings. As they entered, Annalisa's torch went out.

"I think it's the lack of oxygen," she said.

She scrambled in the dark for a moment, but the torchlight was replaced by an eerie glow shining from every direction, illuminating the space sufficiently to see all four corners. The walls were fortified by granite blocks, and the light seemed to come from within the stones themselves. At the opposite side from where they entered, a second doorway connected the room to someplace else.

With nothing to stop the bleeding, Evelyn could not stop the blood from dripping down her arm and onto the floor. The ground vibrated with each drop that landed in dust, shaking the room. The chanting from the townspeople above grew louder, as if they could feel the supernatural energy mounting.

"Shun-kah! Shun-kah! Shun-kah!"

"You're the sacrifice the Masters want," Stewart said, grabbing Evelyn by the hair and pushing her down to her knees. The goheiras hissed loudly at this and stomped their feet in protest.

"Stop!" Grant shouted, twisting Stewart's arm.

Without warning, Ursula fell onto the ground, clutching her head in pain. She kicked and fluttered, her eyes firmly shut, holding the sides of her skull. The fit only lasted seconds, and she stood up again, her robes dusty and disheveled. "There is something that protects her from their influence. For that reason, her sacrifice will mean nothing if she is not willing."

"Willing?" Grant asked.

"To die…" Ursula said, looking over to Fred and Analisa.

Without missing a beat, they picked Evelyn up off the floor. Fred pinned her arms behind her back, leaving her open and undefended.

"Do it," Ursula commanded.

Grant looked away as Analisa began beating Evelyn, drawing blood from her lip and hitting her body with short, cracking punches, rattling her bones. Analisa was almost feral, ecstatic in her violence; Fred was calm and controlled.

Evelyn could see Terry, Casey, and Stewart watching with fascination.

"How can you just watch?" Evelyn cried at Casey. *Adrian, where are you?* she wondered.

CHAPTER 14

ADRIAN WAITED THE hours of the morning at the Riverside Inn, expecting Evelyn to return. Growing more concerned as the time passed, it didn't take long for him to assume the worst, that she'd been taken or killed. Adrian knew Ursula and her team would return to the factory after dark. It was the one thing he could rely on, and he desperately hoped he'd find Evelyn alive there tonight.

Just after the sun went down, Adrian arrived at Dyeworks with a duffle slung around his shoulder and hurried under the clock tower. With the padlock still damaged from his first entry, it was easy for him to hinge the door open and enter. Adrian tiptoed cautiously inside, proceeding toward the back end, walking along the line of dye drums in the center of the hall. Halfway down, he saw them—a group of townspeople standing by the hole in dim light, staring down like zombies, chanting in low octaves.

Hiding behind the pairs of drums to avoid being seen, Adrian snuck into the narrow space between them, inching closer to the crowd with the duffle securely on his back. The pit itself was wider and deeper than before, and a strange glow emanated from its center. Adrian looked for Evelyn, but she wasn't in the crowd, and neither was Ursula or her team. *They must be down there*, he realized.

With no option but to charge past the townspeople and look for Evelyn in the depths, Adrian prepared himself for a battle with both the living and the dead. He unzipped his bag and took out his axe, with the UV lights still attached. Next, he removed a small, battery-powered boombox and placed it on the ground. He positioned the boombox between the dye drums, facing the crowd, hoping to force added resonance and amplification. The audio CD inside was something he'd picked up in his travels through Nepal, a recording of Himalayan monks chanting, invoking compassion. It was a pleasant and soothing sound compared to the dismal hums echoing through the factory.

I hope they hate it, Adrian grinned, pushing play on the stereo set to full volume. The loud and rhythmic Buddhist chanting filled the hall, syncopated with the booming frequencies of a ceremonial gong. The townspeople looked all around for the source of the disruption. Adrian clicked on his UV lights and charged at them, running as fast as he could, axe in hand. He crashed through their ranks, knocking several people onto the floor. There were no goheiras among them, and the hole was only a few feet away. Adrian dangled his legs over the edge and quickly lowered himself into the hole, tightly clutching the axe. He let go and landed hard on his feet before tumbling onto the dirt.

There were two tunnels before him, cut through the rock under the foundation. One led straight ahead into a distant chamber emitting a peculiar glow. The other veered to the right and went deeper into the ground. Getting back up, Adrian spotted a handful of goheiras blocking the entrance a few feet into the first tunnel.

They came at him all at once, scurrying through the dark passageway, running alongside the walls and overhead on the ceiling. Adrian swung his axe repeatedly in all directions, blinding them with flashing UV lights and cutting them down one by one. He used the top side of his axe to bludgeon the ones attacking from above, smashing their bodies into the ceiling. All remains withered and turned to ash.

Clearing the way, Adrian moved forward until he came upon the opening into the next chamber glowing with an eerie light. As soon as he entered, he saw Evelyn standing with her arms pinned behind her back by Fred. In front of her, Analisa stood with her fists up and clenched. A few feet away, Ursula stood with the blood-stained knife in her hands. The others stood idly, their faces twisted with exhilaration, while Evelyn's said despair. She had a cut under her eye, blood running from her nose, and a sizable gash on her forearm.

"Get him!" Ursula shouted as goheiras piled in from the tunnel, amassing around the perimeter.

Fred sprang into action first, releasing Evelyn from his hold. He marched his chubby middle-aged body across the room with his fists up. Adrian cracked him first with the blunt end of his axe right between the eyes. Fred toppled like a tree from the single blow, splitting his head open on the hard rock ground.

Not even Ursula expected the goheira to pounce on his chest and rip his throat open, teeth tearing through flesh and veins. Analisa's scream was deafening. The blood spurted from his neck and collected in a widening pool around his body. The faint sounds from the boombox disappeared. Analisa picked up her extinguished torch, holding it like a club, and stepped toward Adrian. Joining in her fight, Terry reached into his cloak, pulling out a dagger of his own. They both approached Adrian, ready to end his life.

Adrian warned them away, swinging his axe wildly in front of his chest. Annalisa darted back and forth, distracting him, while Terry circled, looking for a way to put a knife in his back. Goheiras nipped at Adrian's ankles. Annalisa managed to slip under Adrian's defense, nearly breaking his nose with her torch. Seeing his opportunity, Terry leaped forward with the knife aimed at Adrian's heart. Evelyn's scream provided the warning he needed.

Instinctually, Adrian raised his axe overhead and turned to bring it down, sinking the sharp metal edge into the side of Terry's neck. The blow nearly severed his head from his body, and the blood erupted like a geyser spraying across the floor. His lifeless body fell face-first into the dirt as Adrian stepped away.

Ursula and Casey's harrowing cries filled the chamber as the goheiras rushed to swarm Terry's body, the way they'd done with Fred's, eating every morsel of flesh off their bones. Without waiting a second longer, Adrian grabbed Evelyn's arm and raced to the second opening at the other end of the room. It wasn't a guaranteed exit, but as they approached, they saw that it led into another tunnel, leading away from the factory. Adrian went in first, using his light to shine the way, holding Evelyn's hand closely at his back.

The tunnel extended into the darkness for a good distance before they noticed a gradual gain in elevation. At the end, they found a narrow shaft going straight up. With the bit of moonlight shining through, Adrian guessed it would lead them right outside. He hoisted Evelyn onto his shoulders and lifted her into the narrow space. She grasped at roots, dirt, and grass, using all her strength to pull her body up and climb out. A minute later, Adrian popped out beside her in the woods, a fair distance away from the factory.

"Are you okay?" Adrian asked, seeing the extent of her wounds up close. Evelyn had blood trickling from a wound under one eye, a severe laceration on her arm, and she was caked with dirt and sweat.

"I'm fine," she said because it was him she was worried about. He'd just killed a man, and she knew it would tear him up eventually.

Before she could offer any words of comfort, Casey emerged from the ground, possessed by rage. She immediately rose to her feet, fixating on Evelyn. Seconds later, Analisa furiously clawed out of the dirt, followed by Grant.

"I'll kill you!" Casey screamed, lunging at her best friend and tackling her into the damp grass. Climbing on top of her, Casey placed her hands around Evelyn's neck and started squeezing the way Hendrick had once strangled her. Starved for oxygen, Evelyn desperately tried to pry Casey's fingers away, panicking, kicking her legs violently. Unable to fight back.

A few feet away, Annalisa held the torch in her hand. She lit the end and stepped forward, ready to kill Adrian for what he'd done to two members of her team. Grant grabbed her arm and pulled her back.

"Give that to me," he said, taking the weapon from her hand. "I want to see what this guy can do."

Switching positions with Annalisa, Grant approached Adrian, holding the flaming torch like a sword. Adrian swung his axe, but Grant did not flinch. Displaying his fencing ability, he deflected Adrian's strikes, whacking him hard between swings. Though several years older, it was easy for Grant to dance around Adrian's clumsy movements before knocking the axe out of his hand.

Adrian didn't miss a beat. He balled his fist behind his back and threw an overhand right, using his height and long arms to cover the distance. The punch flew past the burning stick and landed in the center of Grant's face, sending shock waves rippling through his cheeks. He toppled into the patch of weeds at their side, knocked out cold.

Adrian picked up his axe just as Analisa jumped forward to grab ahold of it and attempted to wrestle it away from him. He towered over her and delivered a headbutt to the bridge of her nose that shook her skull, knocking her down. Feeling the rage bubble up inside, he took his axe and raised it overhead, ready to cut Annalisa in half. That's when he noticed Evelyn on the ground, being choked by Casey and gasping for life.

He ran over to them and looped his hands around Casey's shoulders, pulling her off Evelyn, who immediately gulped in air. Casey jerked violently, fighting to get out of the clench, but he held her tightly. Adrian could feel the darkness inside, compelling her to madness.

"Put your hands on her and think of a memory only you two can remember," Adrian said hurriedly, trying to keep Casey still.

With no time to ask why, Evelyn did as he asked and took Casey's face in her hands. She closed her eyes and held an image of them as innocent children in her mind, standing together in a sunny classroom, smiling at each other. This was the first time they met when they were nine years old, and Casey had just moved to Baneford. "We've always been friends. This isn't you," Evelyn sighed, hoping to transmit all the love she could.

Adrian focused his attention on Casey's heart and could sense the darkness moving away, her true self beginning to shine through. They continued to pour their good energy into her until her face softened, and Adrian felt her resistance diminish, then stop. When Evelyn let her go, it was the real Casey that stepped forward. Tears collected at the corners of her eyes. She took several deep breaths and looked around the woods as if waking up from a dream.

"We have to go now," Adrian said, pointing, "deeper into the woods."

Nearby, Grant and Annalisa began to move around in the grass, a sign they would soon be getting up. The sound of goheiras clicking echoed out of the hole in the ground.

"Casey, we have to get out of here; come with us," Evelyn pleaded, looking into her friend's eyes.

"Okay."

The three of them ran, disappearing between the trees. They continued at a fast pace for a few minutes before daring to stop and turn around. When they finally did, they were alone. From there, Adrian slowed their pace to a brisk walk, and they came out of the woods near the banks of the river. Walking north against the current, they came upon the gas station on Gould Street, where they found a taxi to take them to safety.

"Where can we go?" Evelyn asked nervously, opening the door to the backseat.

"I think it is best to leave town," Adrian answered, taking the evening's events strongly into consideration. Before either of them could think of a hotel, Casey suggested an alternate idea.

"Let's go to my parent's house," Casey said. "They're out of town for a while. It'll be the easiest option."

Evelyn and Adrian exchanged glances. It was a familiar option, but it was impossible to know whether they could trust Casey. Adrian hoped that their combined effort to bring her back permanently had worked and, with that, agreed. They were already dirty, bloody, and far too conspicuous to travel far. Casey gave the address, and the taxi crossed over into the next town, where the streets were instantly prettier, the roads smoother, and the homes much more expensive.

Casey's family lived in an updated Georgian colonial home guarded by tall metal fences and a wrought iron gate. Towering evergreens ran alongside the fencing, creating privacy. With over five thousand square feet of living space, at times, it seemed more like an estate than a house to Evelyn, who'd grown up in much humbler accommodations. Casey used the keys in her pocket to unlock the front door.

"Where is your family?" Evelyn asked, stepping inside.

"They're in Aruba," Casey said, holding back a smile. "Please, make yourselves at home."

It was typical of her to see the humor in the situation, given the contrast between where she was and where her parents were at this moment. But instead of seeing the authenticity in Casey's smile, Evelyn panicked about trusting her so soon. Adrian did not seem to share the concern, opening the liquor cabinet to pour a glass of whiskey. He sat at a table in the study to finish the drink and waited for his nerves to settle.

Casey grabbed Evelyn's hand, pulling her into the kitchen.

"Evie, I can't even begin to say how sorry I am."

"It's not your fault."

"It feels like it was all a dream, but I know it happened."

"It happened," Evelyn repeated with a sad tone. "And I'm sorry too…."

When Adrian joined them, he asked Casey to bring peroxide and bandages. She watched as he tended to the cuts on Evelyn's forearm and face, disinfecting and then dressing the wounds with steady hands. It was obvious in his every movement that he loved her. Evelyn feared how Casey would see it so soon after Terry's death. They were not affectionate openly, but their invisible love was impossible not to see.

"I've got nothing left," Evelyn said, having suffered a long day. "I need to lie down and rest."

Casey showed them to one of the guest bedrooms on the second floor with twin beds, cheerful blue curtains, and a private bath. "I'll see you in the morning," she whispered, disappearing down the hallway to her old room.

CHAPTER 15

IN THE MIDDLE of the night, Casey snuck into the guest room. She stood between the twin beds looking down at her friends, breathing deeply in their sleep, knocked out by stress and exhaustion. Wearing only her underwear, Casey climbed on top of Adrian, straddling his warm body.

"I bet you've thought about this, haven't you?" Casey whispered in his ear, placing her palms against his bare chest.

Before he could say a word, Adrian heard the front door of the house crashing down and footsteps marching furiously up the stairs. Startled awake, Evelyn peered over and saw Casey's half-naked body on top of Adrian, and she heard the incoming footsteps. Grant and Analisa stormed into the room and flicked on the lights, with Stewart trailing in behind them.

"I called my friends," Casey said, eyeing Evelyn and speaking in a tone that indicated she was pleased with herself.

Grant's eyes were both blackened and swollen. Annalisa wore the bulk of her bruising across the bridge of her broken nose. The sight of them looking like raccoons could have made Evelyn laugh had Grant not brought a gun. With the pistol pointed at Evelyn's head, Adrian saw there was little he would be able to do. Not wasting any time, Grant and Analisa steered them out of the room. Adrian and Evelyn dawdled through the house at gunpoint, groggy, frustrated, and utterly exhausted. A much-needed reprieve from the insanity would not be coming soon. Evelyn looked over at Adrian and sensed the defeat.

Summoned back to Dyeworks, Evelyn and Adrian reentered the factory through the back wall, at gunpoint, with Grant and Analisa walking closely behind. There were still people gathered, including Mayor Jenkins and Chief Rawlings, unbothered by the late hour of night. Evelyn could see by the emptiness in their eyes how deeply entranced they were. Ursula's cloak was stained and torn from her climb back to ground level. She stood before the townspeople, praising the Masters with an air of desperation.

"Their wisdom is ancient, their power greater than we can imagine."

The crowd responded with low octave chants, "Shun-kah, Shun-kah, Shun-kah."

"And their sacrifice has arrived!" she said as Evelyn and Adrian reluctantly entered the hall.

Ursula leered at Adrian as he passed before her, taking in his impressive stature for the first time.

"He's different," Stewart whispered to her. "He knows things."

"Let's see what his soul is worth," she said, grabbing Adrian's arm and pushing back his sleeve.

Ursula extended his arm over the hole, unsheathed her knife, and drew blood from his forearm, letting it drip down onto the heads of the goheiras below. They erupted into a flurry of competition, snapping their jaws at the trickle of Adrian's blood, squealing with delight.

"See!" Stewart said as the townspeople looked at Adrian with awe.

"I think you're right," Ursula said, admiring her prize. She ran the tip of her index finger across his lips, eyeing Evelyn. "What makes you so special?"

"He loves her," Casey said. "And he's a medium. He can speak to the dead."

"Then maybe he's the reason the Masters cannot reach either of them," Ursula replied.

"He killed Fred and Terry," Annalisa said bitterly from behind her busted nose.

"Sacrifice him first!" Stewart shouted.

"Who are you?" she asked Adrian, holding the knife to his throat. "How do you know this woman?"

Adrian kept his mouth shut and looked away, refusing to answer her. The truth, however, was he wasn't sure why the influence hadn't affected Evelyn, though it was certainly creeping in on him. He felt the burning anger inside mounting quickly, threatening to blot out the true version of himself. *She will be alone,* he realized, with the darkness closing in like a curtain.

"If you won't talk, we'll beat it out of you. Then the Masters can have your soul," Ursula sneered.

The moment Grant stepped forward, took off his sport coat, and gave his gun to Ursula, Adrian felt the intense desire to tear him apart, and it was a vile, murderous impulse coursing through his veins. He squared off with Grant, taking no pause to reconsider an invitation to fight to the death. Evelyn feared he would not win. Adrian had the height and size advantage, but Grant was not an easy opponent. Coached by elite trainers for decades, changing disciplines over the years, Grant had considerable experience with hand-to-hand combat techniques and the conditioning to withstand most physical challenges. He was fit, intelligent, and well-trained.

Both of Grant's eyes were blackened, his face was bruised, and there were scrapes on his hands and arms, but there was no fear expressed on his face. Twisted by a lust for power, influenced by the primitive and bestial energy of the Masters, he lunged at Adrian, tackling him at the waist. They crashed onto the concrete floor, viciously punching each other, feet from the harrowing pit. The townspeople watched from the other side with vacant stares like mindless passengers on a city bus. Managing to get on top of him, Grant punched down at Adrian's face with everything he had. If it weren't for Adrian's long arms pushing him back, creating distance, he would have succeeded in knocking his teeth out. But Adrian slipped away and stood up, where his reach could make a bigger difference.

Adrian threw out lengthy snapping jabs, one after the other, striking Grant's face, making it nearly impossible for him to get close. Provoked to hatred, Grant walked into the punches, taking hard hits to the head. On the inside, he unleashed a barrage of short cracking punches to Adrian's ribs, making him grimace from pain.

Then the change happened, and Adrian slipped away entirely. Evelyn saw it in his eyes the moment he disappeared. Ursula smiled because she saw it too. Adrian forced his elbow into the side of Grant's face, dislocating his jaw. The hard right that followed rattled his bones, and Grant's legs collapsed underneath him. Adrian viciously launched his boot into Grant's ribs, forcing him to shrivel and cower on the ground. He kicked him again, then again, and again.

"I will kill you!" Adrian screamed, and Evelyn's stomach turned, witnessing the Masters' cruelty.

Grant's ribs were broken, his face unrecognizable, and he barely moved. Adrian grabbed him by the hair and bashed his head against the side of the metal drum, cracking his skull open. When the body dropped, a goheira climbed out of the hole, its leathery face hanging over the edge, eyeing the freshly served pink and red meat.

"Well done," Ursula laughed, clapping her hands loudly. "Come, come."

Adrian stepped away from Grant's body as more of the beasts crawled out from the pit, scurrying across the floor to eat. To Evelyn's horror, he joined Ursula by her side, with blood splattered across his face, chest still heaving from the fight.

"What is your name?"

"Adrian."

"Perhaps you're worth keeping," Ursula said, resting her hand on his tall shoulder.

"You're not going to kill him?" Stewart screamed.

"We still don't know what makes her so special," she said, turning to face Evelyn. "Let's see how badly she wants to live."

Evelyn feared she'd be fighting Casey, which she could not do. Fortunately, it was Annalisa that stepped forward. She ran at Evelyn, screaming, with her fists in the air. In an instant, she was on top of her, hammering her over the head. Evelyn cowered under the blows, trying to protect herself.

Unable to hit Annalisa even once, Evelyn backed away. She retreated right up to the hole, her heels practically hanging over the edge. Analisa came forward swinging, throwing her weight into her attack. Evelyn ducked and spun around, popping up right behind Analisa. She kicked her as hard as she could, and Analisa went flying back-first into the dark pit.

From above, they heard the loud thud and the desperate gasps for air, followed by the sound of wet flesh being gnawed. For the first time, Ursula looked at Evelyn with fear in her own eyes. Four people from her team were dead, and she'd failed to procure an appropriate sacrifice. But she directed her anger at the crowd gathered in the dark hall.

"All of you! Get out!" Ursula barked, commanding them to leave the factory. "None of your souls have any value here!"

Slowly, some in the crowd began to disperse, with others, like Mayor Jenkins and Casey, lingering behind, apprehensive about what to do.

"I said get out!" she screamed at them.

Startled, they turned to follow the rest of the herd waddling through the large hall and out of sight.

Even without the townspeople, Ursula still had Stewart, the goheiras, and now Adrian on her side. The night wasn't over yet, and Evelyn believed that either she or Adrian would be offered so the Masters could have at least one special soul.

"A lot of people are dead because of you," Ursula seethed at her.

"Does that mean the Masters failed you?" Evelyn replied, finding the courage to stand up for herself. Ursula's eyes opened wide. They were bloodshot and filled with longing. Evelyn could see the intensity of her desire, how badly she wanted the Masters' favor.

"It means I'm going to enjoy killing you," she said, walking around Adrian, running her hands over his shoulders. "Bring her down."

Ursula turned to see Evelyn's green eyes the moment Adrian grasped the back of her shirt, shoving her forward.

"Adrian? What are you doing?" she pleaded.

The three of them stood at the edge of the hole, looking down at the sea of goheiras. Adrian lowered Evelyn in, dropping her the last several feet. The goheiras parted as she collapsed onto the dirt floor. Adrian, Ursula, and Stewart followed, forcing her through the tunnel to the inner chamber. Goheiras scuttled around them, making way for the Masters' sacrifice. Passing through the darkness, they entered the granite room with the mysterious light emitted from within the walls.

241

Ursula grabbed Evelyn by the hair and dragged her to the center of the room. "Kneel!" she said, pushing her onto her knees. "You as well," Ursula commanded Adrian.

He set his large body down beside Evelyn without protest. Stewart peered down at them with a vengeance in his heart, grinding his jaw and spasming like an epileptic on meth. Ursula unsheathed her dagger and placed the blade on Evelyn's neck, its sharpness drawing the thinnest red line across her throat. Stewart's heavy breathing filled her ears. The goheiras stomped their heels into the dirt, hissing loudly.

"Why?" Ursula shouted at them. "What makes her so important?"

Evelyn felt a slight rumbling underneath her feet, and the tremor intensified quickly. The room shook, and dust filled the air as the ground cracked open. What started as a hairline fracture quickly widened, running across the chamber floor, and turned into a deep chasm, nearly splitting the room in half. The quaking ground knocked Ursula off balance, sending the gun tumbling down into the black abyss. From where they knelt, only feet away from the widest part of the chasm, Evelyn could see that the depths reached far into the subterranean darkness, where she surmised the Masters were waiting.

Ursula regained her footing and held her ground at the precipice, feeling the Masters' bloodlust in the rising hot air. They desired Evelyn's soul with a burning hunger, seeking to dominate her will. No one understood why. But Ursula had a suspicion it was because Evelyn's soul was so pure, and her love was so strong and unconditional, and she was right. Evelyn felt love for the ones closest to her so deeply that the Masters could not corrupt her heart. As it had been before with Hendrick, her heart was the magnet that drew evil in and simultaneously the shield that protected her from harm.

Ursula put her theory to the test by placing her blade against Adrian's throat instead. She looked to the crimson creatures lining the perimeter for a sign, and they stared back at her through their slit eyes, jaws gaping open, ready to shovel wet flesh into their leathery faces. Not one of them hissed in disapproval, and it was a good sign of the Masters' consent.

"If your love stands in the way of the Masters' sacrifice, then I'll remove it," Ursula said, threatening to kill Adrian.

He made no protestations, resting on his knees, staring straight ahead, willing, at any moment, to let Ursula cut his throat. Evelyn reached out and squeezed his hand. He gave her nothing in return. His eyes were empty, and he looked at her as if he'd never seen her before.

"Wait! Let him go," Evelyn pleaded. "I'll do it if you leave him alone."

"Finally!" Stewart whined.

Ursula smiled and pressed the point of her blade over Evelyn's heart, lightly pressing it into her skin.

"A knife through the heart for you."

She looked to the goheiras, who stomped their feet in celebration, grinding their jaws into twisted grins. Accepting her time to die, Evelyn turned to Adrian one last time to say all the things she should have said before—the same words she'd wanted to hear from him. *At least one of us can say it,* she reasoned, *even if it is too late.*

"I love you, Adrian," she said, brushing the tears from her eyes. "This isn't how I wanted it to be for us. I wish we had more time. It just wasn't enough… You risked your life for me, my friends, and for this town countless times. I thought I'd have a lifetime to show you how much it meant, but I only have this moment. I love you, Adrian, and I happily give my life to save yours. I hope you finally find your home." Seeing no response in his face, Evelyn closed her eyes and waited for Ursula's knife. "Perhaps in the next life, we'll be together," she sighed, wondering if she'd see her parents again. Stewart frothed with exhilaration. Unexpectedly, Adrian turned to Evelyn. From the corner of his eye, he saw the knife moving and threw his body forward, taking the knife for her.

Evelyn heard his tortured gasp, and her eyes popped open to see Adrian's body thud onto the ground at her side by the precipice. He clutched his bleeding chest, moaning from the pain, his hands overflowing with blood. The goheiras hissed but showed odd restraint. Had Maruf been there, he would have rejoiced, expecting Adrian's curse to be gone. There were three parts to the ritual, and Evelyn had unknowingly performed them with sincerity and purpose. Ursula dropped the bloody dagger and clutched her head, bellowing from the sudden pressure inside. Stewart could barely stand from the intensifying spasms rippling up his spine.

Adrian wearily looked down into the empty chasm from where he lay on the ground and sensed the Masters hiding below. He could not see them at first, but he heard them. They shouted in an unknown language across the expanse. Adrian felt their energy, and it was primitive and evil. They were hungry, vicious spirits, banished to the depths as the consequence of their vile ways.

"You betrayed me!" Ursula screeched at Adrian.

"It is they who have betrayed you," he said between labored gasps. "Let me show you what you've always wanted to see."

Adrian lifted himself back onto his knees. The goheiras watched, still as statues. He closed his eyes, placed his hands in his lap, and let the voices in, listening to their insanity, allowing their emotions to penetrate his heart. He felt their yearning and despair, and it reminded him of Hendrick and his insatiable lust for blood. A vision began to form in Adrian's mind.

Chief Annawan appeared, his long black hair tucked under a crown of feathers, wearing the symbol of the coyote on his skins. Adrian felt the man's sadness, the awful pain that only a grieving parent would know. But Annawan let out deep, thunderous laughter from his belly, and Adrian tasted bittersweet satisfaction for vengeance being served. Adrian saw that it was a curse. Just as Annawan's wife and daughter suffered the fever that took them, so, too, would the daughters of the invading Europeans find their anguish in ancient curses as retribution for the diseases their fathers brought to the New World.

Ursula looked on suspiciously. Evelyn saw the shuddering in Adrian's body and the fluttering of his eyelids. She could not imagine what it was he saw, but she noticed the change in his posture as he went deeper into the trance.

All shapes and colors coalesced into a single point, hurtling through an ocean of collective memory. It raced backward through history, crossing millennia, and crashed into a distant past. Adrian saw a village nestled against the banks of a mighty river. He sensed blood magic on every road, in every home, and in every soul who lived there. Suffering under the weight of this evil, the earth cracked open and swallowed the village whole. That evil's name was "Shun-kah." Twisted by time, spilling out of the earth with hunger, the Masters found new blood and lingered on.

When Adrian opened his eyes, he saw the many spirits of the Masters in the depths of the chasm. Scores of them, nearly absent of form and color, floated up out of the darkness into the glowing chamber. They appeared as whisps of smoke, spun loosely in the shapes of the people they once were. As the ghosts drifted past, Adrian saw by their mutilated faces and disfigured parts that blood magic had ruined their souls.

The spirits ascended to the ceiling and amassed there, growing in number, looking down upon Ursula, Stewart, and Evelyn. Ursula wept from sorrow as the sounds of chanting filled the chamber, emanating from the Masters themselves, vibrating the air.

"Shun-kah... Shun-kah... Shun-kah," they repeated, honoring their lost world.

"These are not the gods you expected," Evelyn said. Ursula wailed, gazing at the ceiling, devastated by the harsh truth she saw.

The Masters were old, eroded beings, tethered to this world by blood magic alone. These spirits did not possess any real wisdom, nor did their actions hold meaning. They were nothing but hungry ghosts, trading pieces of themselves to feed an insatiable need brought on by their curse.

"None of this was meant as a gift," Adrian said. "Annawan knew there was evil here. This was his revenge. The Masters don't give power, they take it. Blood magic offers only false promises because it destroys the soul."

Ursula looked up at the ancient spirits floating above with great regret in her eyes, finally seeing her Masters as they really were, far from the benevolent beings she had hoped them to be. The goheiras hissed and growled at her because the Masters sensed her betrayal.

"And what do you expect me to do after showing me this?" Ursula said, kicking Adrian in the chest, knocking him back down off his knees. He grasped at his chest, and the blood continued to leak through his shirt. Ursula kicked him again, almost rolling him straight over the edge into the chasm below. "If my life has meant nothing, then yours will too!" she screamed.

Evelyn saw she would lose him. Adrian desperately scratched at the ground, trying to hold on to keep from falling in. Evelyn grabbed Ursula's dagger from the ground, leaped up, and plunged the blade deep into her eye socket.

Using it as an anchor in her skull, she pulled her forward and flung her at the crevasse in the ground. Ursula's body flopped over the edge and disappeared into the darkness. At once, the spirits circling overhead shot back down into the chasm, leaving the chamber. The goheiras ran toward the black void in the ground, coming from every direction, tossing their bodies over the edge.

"Help me lift him up," Evelyn implored Stewart.

Puzzled for a moment as if released from a trance, Stewart stared at her, then at Adrian's bleeding chest, before deciding to help. Together, they got Adrian onto his feet. It hurt him to breathe, but he carried forward, back through the tunnel to the pit in the floor of Dyeworks. Evelyn climbed out first, and Stewart helped Adrian climb up the dirt walls. At the top, Evelyn took his hands and pulled as hard she could to bring him up. The three of them walked through the dark, silent factory, past the long line of dye drums, toward the front entrance.

They exited under the clock tower at the latest hour of night when normally no one would be outside. They saw a blue SUV parked across the street, with its lights and engine on. The driver rolled the window down, and it was Casey behind the wheel.

"Get in!" she said, getting out of the car to help.

"He needs a hospital," Evelyn said, easing Adrian into the passenger side before getting in the back.

"Don't worry, they're gone," Casey said, peeling away, leaving Stewart standing alone on the empty street.

"I know," Evelyn replied.

CHAPTER 16

ADRIAN STRUGGLED TO breathe at Old Bedford Hospital, coughing up blood and wheezing through fluid-filled lungs. Seeing his condition as critical, the doctors rushed him to surgery, leaving a single nurse behind to accompany Evelyn and Casey to the attendant physician in urgent care. Casey only had a few minor cuts and scrapes on her body, hardly in need of professional attention, but the swelling of Evelyn's face and the cuts under her eye and on her forearm looked ugly under the fluorescent light. When asked how they'd sustained the injuries, Evelyn gave an unlikely story about being mugged. Judging by the doctors' expressions, they didn't believe the story but treated and discharged them, nonetheless.

Bandaged and deemed healthy, Evelyn and Casey checked out and immediately went to find Adrian. The stab wound in his chest had cost him a significant amount of blood, and they feared what news they might hear. Arriving on his floor an hour after his surgery, they waited in the lounge outside the recovery room, where an ER physician eventually came to meet them. He was a young doctor, not much older than them, clean-shaven with a baby face.

"We just performed a minor surgery to drain his pleural cavity and stop the hemorrhaging. We believe he'll be okay."

"Thank you, Doctor. Can we see him?" Casey asked.

"We'll need to keep him overnight and most likely a few days more. No visitation now, but you can try tomorrow," the doctor said, offering a friendly half-smile before turning to leave.

It wasn't the news she wanted, but Evelyn accepted it, and they exited the waiting room.

"Come back with me to my parent's house," Casey suggested, and Evelyn agreed.

They arrived at the house just as the sun was coming up. They ate waffles at the dining room table and finally spoke as friends.

"How are people supposed to recover from this?" Casey asked.

"We'll be fine," Evelyn said confidently, pouring more syrup onto her plate.

"Are you crazy? Baneford's fucked. People are probably waking up right now wondering what the hell they've been doing."

"They won't remember what happened. Only a few of us will," Evelyn said, with the conviction of already knowing.

Casey didn't understand, but she was too tired and too overwhelmed to figure it out now. At some point soon, someone would ask about the Hyde Properties team and their mysterious disappearance, and Casey could not imagine what Evelyn could possibly say in response. Nonetheless, after they finished eating, they agreed to rest first and worry later.

Casey went to her room and drew the curtains to shut out the light. Evelyn returned to the room she'd shared with Adrian and hugged the pillow to sleep. Several hours later, in the early afternoon, Casey woke to find Evelyn already in the kitchen drinking her coffee. She poured Casey a cup, and they held their mugs, looking out the window at the budding trees outside as birds hopped from branch to branch, chirping for their mates.

"How do you feel?" Evelyn asked.

"I don't know what to feel. I remember what happened, but it's like I was watching and didn't care. I want you to know that I don't blame you about Terry. I guess I didn't really know him, and you and Adrian did what you had to do."

"I'm sorry. I never wanted you to get hurt, yet somehow, you're always right at the center of whatever trouble I'm in."

"This time, it really isn't your fault…. Are you okay?" Casey asked, pointing at Evelyn's bruised cheek.

"Just very sore."

Casey reached out and hugged her friend, mindful not to squeeze too tight.

"Last night, something told me to go wait outside the factory in the middle of the night because you needed me," Casey said. "I've never experienced anything like that before."

"There's something I need to tell you," Evelyn started, "the Masters spoke to me. They showed me that if I killed

Ursula, I would have a chance to make things right. Adrian was hanging on by a thread, and I had to kill her to save him. I stabbed Ursula in the eye and watched her body fall beyond reach."

"What did you do?" Casey asked, her eyes widening with concern.

"I changed things, starting with you knowing to wait outside," Evelyn said. "I made everyone forget what they did and saw these past several weeks. Only a few of us will remember what really happened."

"Why did you do that?" Casey asked.

"Because people can't know the truth. It would ruin them—and our town."

Casey took some time to think about what was said. It wasn't easy to accept or uphold a lie, but the truth was impossible to believe. After Casey took her shower, got dressed, and packed some of the clothes she'd left behind at her parent's house, she drove Evelyn to her apartment. By the time they went back to Old Bedford hospital, it was late in the afternoon.

In the recovery wing, they found Adrian awake in his room. He lay on the bed in a blue johnny watching a small television, sipping milk through a straw. He smiled when he saw them, like a small boy with his ice cream after a tonsillectomy. Evelyn threw her arms around his neck.

"Does it hurt?" she asked, seeing the bandages where the knife had penetrated his chest.

"Not as much as before."

One of his doctors entered the room to adjust the saline drip. "Since you're doing well, we can release you early this evening, provided you do not aggravate the wound."

"Thank you, Doctor," Adrian replied, appearing quite relaxed.

As the administrators processed Adrian's discharge from the hospital, Evelyn and Casey waited by his side, next to the beeping monitors, making no mention of Dyeworks or the day before. Evelyn reflected on how this experience compared to the one from months ago when Adrian had checked out of the hospital and left town without a word. She wondered what he would do this time, given that his work was now officially over.

When the time came, Adrian walked out of the hospital and went back with them to Evelyn's apartment, where she invited him to stay for a few days.

"That is very kind of you. I will stay," he said with gratitude.

That evening, Evelyn and Casey prepared a meal together while Adrian rested in the living room chair, content to sit quietly and alone. At dinner time, he joined them at the table and appeared to be in a pleasant mood but said little during the meal.

At the end of the night, insisting Casey stay as well, Evelyn prepared the sofa for her and brought Adrian to her room. In bed, he lay with his arm around her, but he did not speak a word. Evelyn didn't know the reason for his silence, though she feared telling him what she'd done.

Evelyn had no way of knowing that she'd inadvertently performed the ritual Maruf received from the Syrians, freeing him of his curse. The voices of the dead would no longer torment his mind if he did not invite them in. When Adrian woke up in the hospital, he noticed silence where there should have been great noise. This was a hospital where people came to die. He sensed the absence of voices might be more than just a reprieve. Something was different. The spirits were not merely quiet but gone altogether. He dared not believe it, that he could finally be free.

Evelyn knew she had to tell Adrian about her deal with the Masters. Cradled in his arms, she could not make herself speak the words, and her heartbeat quickened from nervousness. Adrian felt it thudding against his chest, but he did not speak, keeping his arm wrapped securely around her body.

The next morning, Evelyn sat with Adrian and Casey in the kitchen and knew it was time. Evelyn told Adrian the truth and watched his heart sink. She explained that she'd heard the Masters in her head. In exchange for Ursula's life, they offered something she could not refuse—a way to save him and the town.

"My heart made the deal," she said in conclusion.

Adrian did not preach or lecture because he didn't have to. Evelyn had heard the stories from him before, how dark magic was the death of the soul. She could see by the veins in his neck and the temperature of his skin how much this news troubled him.

"So, what do you imagine happens next?" Adrian asked.

"I have a plan. We're going to see the mayor."

Adrian looked at Casey with profound confusion, hoping to receive an explanation but heard none. After breakfast, they ventured out in Casey's car; things seemed fine in Baneford. A normal, uneventful Monday morning. Pedestrians walked the streets in the fair weather, cars rolled past in good order, and everyone had remembered to bring their trash and recycling bins out to the curb.

When they arrived at city hall, Evelyn told security she had an urgent message for Mayor Jenkins. An assistant she hadn't seen before came to greet them in the lobby and brought them up. They crossed the red carpet to the door of the mayor's office and went inside. Mayor Jenkins sat alone behind his desk, staring down at his knees. He looked up when he saw Evelyn and frowned.

"I can explain everything that's happened," she said, approaching his desk.

"There's no way you can explain it because it doesn't make any fucking sense!" The mayor shouted, his face turning red.

"I know you're upset and confused. Sit down with me, and I promise, if you can believe what I tell you, you'll understand, and it won't be as bad as you think." Evelyn spoke confidently in a calm way that grabbed Adrian and Casey's attention, too.

"Fine," the mayor huffed, pointing at the round table near the corner of the room.

"Everyone, sit down, please. I've also asked a few others to join us." Evelyn confidently took control of the situation.

"Others who?" the mayor asked as Adrian and Casey took their seats at the round table.

The office door popped open, and Stewart's yellow head appeared in the narrow crack. He looked around cautiously before walking into the room.

"I don't want to see *him*!" the mayor barked. "He's the one who fucked this up in the first place."

"I know, Mayor. Wait."

The door opened again, and it was Chief Rawlings. He looked frightened and disheveled, but Evelyn welcomed him to the table. He sat down, darting his eyes curiously at everyone else. They all stared at her, waiting for an explanation for why they'd been summoned.

"I asked everyone here so you can hear the truth. The town was cursed, and almost everyone in it was under a spell. Today, you're remembering the things you said and did the last few weeks and wondering if it was real," she said, speaking to the mayor and the chief. "Those memories are real, and you're not going crazy." Evelyn took a moment to assess their reactions. She needed them to play a pivotal role in her plan, and it would require their complete understanding and cooperation. She studied every emotion flashing across their faces.

"Ursula drugged us. Is that it?" the mayor asked.

"It might seem that way, but there were no drugs. You were under a spell."

"You expect us to believe that?" Chief Rawlings bellowed at her, slamming his fist down on the table.

Adrian and Casey watched Evelyn manage the situation, displaying shrewdness and a knack for persuasion they did not know she possessed.

"You saw Ursula kill people from our town… you saw those red creatures eat their bodies… and you saw me, and this man, kill two members of their team Saturday night," she said, gesturing at Adrian.

The mayor and chief looked at each other, confounded.

"That really happened?" the mayor asked, swallowing hard.

"And we watched and did nothing," the chief said softly.

"I know about the deal you did with Hyde Properties. You sold town assets for personal gain, and you listened to him," she said, pointing in Stewart's direction. "You chose wrong, but that's not what this is about."

"We could have transformed the town!" Stewart interjected.

"Shut up!" Adrian commanded, reducing him to a puddle of fear in his seat.

It took her some time, but Evelyn explained why Ursula wanted Dyeworks and what the power underneath the factory really was. They were appalled and struggled to believe the story, but the number of dead residents was impossible to ignore, and neither were their odd, disjointed memories.

"Ed Crowley is dead because of this. Your cousin and colleague, but he wasn't the only one. Sam, Sheryl, Mr. Bluff, Mr. Moulton... they're all gone."

Chief Rawlings rubbed his neck and ears furiously while Mayor Jenkins sat beside him, grinding his jaw and grimacing from recollection. Stewart gripped the side of the table with both hands, leaning forward with anticipation, holding back the involuntary spasms in his body, desperately waiting to see what Evelyn intended to do with Ursula's work.

"I killed Ursula," Evelyn said finally. "But I'm not the only one who's committed crimes. You illegally sold town assets. You turned a blind eye and let the murders happen on your watch."

"You'll never prove any of that!" the mayor said.

"I'm not here to fight you or seek justice. I want to erase the whole thing. When Ursula died, we got a chance to set things right. That's why we are the only ones who will remember what happened. That's how we can use the power at Dyeworks to help our town."

"And you can do that; how?" the chief asked.

"Leave that to me. But I promise you, no one outside this room will remember any of it."

Adrian could hardly believe what he was hearing. His face turned white, and deep lines formed over his brow.

"You are using blood magic to change history," he said, shaking his head in judgment.

"As for the dead or missing," Evelyn continued, "the police department and the mayor's office will jointly announce that the bodies of the missing persons were found at the scene of an accident at the old factory."

"What accident?" Casey inquired.

"We're going to burn Dyeworks down."

Everyone looked at Evelyn as if they'd never seen her before. Adrian was the first to respond.

"I agree that it must be destroyed."

"No!" Stewart screamed, banging his fist on the table. "You can't destroy it! Don't you understand what that means!"

"Shut your mouth! If it weren't for you and your insane idea, none of this would have happened, and my cousin would be alive. Get out; you're fired!" The mayor shouted at him.

He followed Stewart all the way from his seat to the door and watched him shuffle out of the room before slamming the door shut behind him.

"What about you two?" the chief asked, directing his question at Casey and Adrian. "You agree to do what she's saying?"

It was right then that Adrian and Casey really understood the choice Evelyn made. Faced with having to make a choice of their own, they considered what would happen if everyone in town did remember what happened. It would destroy families, lives, and businesses and possibly trigger a national emergency—the loser town that went bat shit crazy. Everyone would assume it was a chemical attack or a religious cult gone mad, and no one would think of the town in any other way for decades to come. A silence ensued, wherein they all looked at each other to find the consensus, and it was clear.

"How do we blow it up?" the mayor asked.

"We'll take care of that. Meet us at Dyeworks in two hours," Evelyn said, standing up from her seat.

With her back to the window, the light from outside formed a halo around her head. Adrian and Casey got up and followed her out of the office. Two hours later, they arrived outside Dyeworks, with Casey's car filled with gasoline canisters stacked and tucked neatly under a blanket.

This time, Evelyn asked Casey to head to the back of the property, drive directly onto the lot, and pull up near the demolished wall. Bringing her SUV to the edge of the rubble, Casey opened the gate, and they took turns carrying the jugs into the empty hall, placing them in front of the hole. Wrapping up, Casey parked on the street, and they found Mayor Jenkins and Chief Rawlings standing by the front entrance. With the white clock tower above pointing to the sky, Evelyn grieved for the piece of history and architecture that would be destroyed.

"Meet us out back," she said to them, and they followed her around to the missing wall.

Adrian saw how both the mayor and chief scanned the ground in fear, looking for the goheiras from their memories. "The red ones only come out at night," he assured them.

They stepped over the rubble and walked up to the hole and the cargo of gasoline placed beside the long line of dye drums running to the other end of the factory.

"So, how do we do this?" the mayor asked.

Evelyn looked to Adrian for the answer.

"Begin pouring them on and underneath these dye drums," he said, banging on the closest ones. The rest will spread out over the floor."

"Why the drums?" Casey asked.

"There's old lacquer in those drums. If it gets hot enough, it will explode, and so will the gasoline."

They did as he instructed, spilling gasoline throughout the factory. Adrian covered the second floor and poured gasoline along the aisle and in each of the offices. Evelyn emptied an entire canister directly into the pit. When they were done, they stood overlooking the wet floor and machines, breathing in the potent fumes.

Adrian turned to Evelyn. "Did you ask the Masters to change things for me?"

"No. Change what?"

"I am different. The voices of the dead no longer torment me," he said, barely believing his own words.

"The voices are gone—"

"What now?" the mayor interrupted.

"We can do the rest from outside," Adrian said to him.

He led the way out of the building, and they followed, with the mayor and the chief trailing behind. Adrian removed a glass bottle from his pocket. It was filled with gasoline and stuffed with a rag. He waited for two junkies to turn the corner before lighting it.

"Chief, the investigation here needs to conclude that it was an accident. You'll say that the people missing were found dead inside. The reason unknown. Mr. Mayor, you stopped the development because of suspicions over environmental contamination. A few days later, the building went up in flames—further evidence of hazardous chemicals on the site."

"You have this all figured out, don't you?" the mayor said dryly. "What do I do with Stewart?"

"I would have him admitted at Northoff Psychiatric Hospital for insanity. Have him tell the doctors about his family."

Adrian hurled a Molotov cocktail through one of the windows, breaking the glass. A fire immediately blazed from one end of the factory to the other, and the flames roared through each section of the building.

"We should leave," the chief said, pulling the mayor away.

Evelyn, Adrian, and Casey left promptly, too, speeding away before the fire reached the lacquer in the drums. Casey drove parallel to the river and stopped by the esplanade, where they could observe the factory. From that distance, the flames appeared as tiny orange lights, and they burned brighter until the sound of an explosion shook the sky like thunder. Black smoke shot into the air, and they watched what remained of the Dyeworks burn to the ground.

"Are the voices really gone?"

"I think they are."

"So, what are you going to do now?" Evelyn asked, her green eyes sparkling in the light.

"I want to stay with you," he said. "I love you. I always have."

Tears came to Evelyn's eyes. He took her in his arms and kissed her. Adrian's heart pounded in his chest. He'd never believed this moment would come. She felt his heartbeat and dared to believe he'd stay. It's what Evelyn had wished for all along. With her face pressed gently against Adrian's sweater, endless possibilities came to mind.

"Hurston Laurent was wrong," she whispered to herself, remembering the memoir. *The darker path was the right choice.*

ABOUT THE AUTHOR

ALI KADEN grew up between the US and Egypt, considering both countries "home." Adopting a broad view of the world, he's endlessly fascinated by the diversity of belief systems, mythologies, and cultures. Expectedly, Ali enjoys introducing multicultural elements into each of his stories. As an author, Ali hopes to bring stories to life that readers find deeply moving, creative, and fun. He believes good literature can save lives, or at the very least, make dark days brighter. Passionate about the craft, he loves to use potent descriptions, captivating metaphors, and varied plot structures in his writing. When he's not working on new stories, he co-manages a real estate business in Boston and spends time with his wife, young daughter, and their loyal terrier, Joyous. A fan of boxing, Ali can also often be found hitting the heavy bag to the *Rocky* soundtrack at his local gym.

Visit Ali Kaden's website for new release and author updates: WWW.ALIKADENBOOKS.COM

9 781088 028612